# The Sara Colson Trilogy

## Book One : Sara's Child

By 

Susan Elle

For

Ursula Publishing UK

Dedication

Barbara,
My friend and my
Staunchest supporter in all things.

Thanks Sis'

Sara's Child



Published by

Ursula Publishing UK





Cover Photograph

© Sebastian Czapnik/Dreamstime.com

ISBN  978-1-910753-00-2

# Other Books by Susan Elle

The Sara Colson Trilogy
Sara's Child
Sara's Loss
Sara's Shame
The above are also available as audiobooks.

Missing : Catherine Colson-Sayers (CCS)
Investigations : Book 1
The Chosen : CCS Investigations : Book 2
Travis : CCS Investigations : Book 3
Deleted :  CCS Investigations : Book 4
Mind Games :  CCS Investigations : Book 5
due out end Aug 2015 – twice the length of previous books.

Broken
Tempest

Love, Lies & Consequences Trilogy
Book One : Love
Book Two : Lies
Book Three : Consequences

Langdon Trilogy
Heart & Home
Heart of a Lion
Heart of Stone

www.susan-elle.com

# Table of Contents

# <u>Chapter One</u>

"Damn it, Ben, why the fuck didn't you tell me you are so far behind?" Catherine rages quietly, making some attempt at control. "This is a big account, and one I don't want to lose."

*Shit! Shit! Shit!*

"I didn't tell you because I knew what you'd do," Ben replies, not looking up, his fingers continuing their feverish dance across his computer keyboard.

"Really...and just what might that be?" Hands on hips, Catherine moves to stand right in front of Ben's desk. *Right then!*

At five feet ten, she cuts an imposing figure and her brilliant blue eyes can stop a man dead in his tracks.

His fingers finally still and Ben sits back to eye Catherine steadily. He has worked for her almost from the start of Compusafe's lowly beginnings out of Catherine's one room bedsit.

She managed on her own for just over a year, but her reputation for innovative thinking and dogged determination to see each job completed to the client's satisfaction, and up to her own exacting standards, meant that the workload became unmanageable. "You'd work until you dropped," he states knowingly. "Just like you did six months ago after Pete' left." Fuck!

Catherine opens her mouth to deny it, but can see Ben's planned retort written plainly across his concerned but firm face. "That was just a temporary glitch," she replies with a dismissive wave of her hand. "Just because I got a little over tired and had to take a few days off doesn't mean I can't cope with a little extra work to get this account back on track." For heaven's sake! Hands back on hips her face set in stone, Catherine narrows her sparkling blue eyes. "Just leave me to make my own decisions about how much bloody work I can or can't cope with...I'm still the damned boss around here!" *Are you listening, matey?*

Ben does not falter under Catherine's withering stare, but instead glares right back at her. "Over tired be damned," he scoffs. "You were mentally and physically exhausted and should have been admitted to the hospital. And would have been," he adds hotly when her eyes fire at his reminder, "if you'd listened to your doctor instead of digging your obstinate heels in."

*Obstinate! I'll give you obstinate!*

Barely able to take a breath, Catherine stands stock still, her anger now all consuming. Ben waits for the explosion, wondering if this time he's gone too far. But Ben's damned if he's just going to sit meekly back and watch her make herself even sicker than the last time. He knows she still isn't back to full health yet, her recovery being slowed down by the fact that she still insists on working the clock round. Well, *she can't fire me,* he reasons silently, *not now it's just the two of us.* At least, that's what he hopes.

*Ha, I get it!* "You think you're safe," Catherine guesses, and knows she is correct when Ben has the grace to blush. "Well don't get too comfortable in that damn awful chair you insisted I buy you." To her eyes, it truly is awful, some new-fangled design meant to help posture and minimise back problems for overworked desk jockeys. And it's bright red, of all things. *Fucking bright, in your face, red!*

Giving herself a mental shake, Catherine's voice lowers to a dangerous hush that tells Ben, she is one-step away from losing it. "Pete may have jumped ship for an easier life but I thought you had more spine than that dickwad. If I was wrong," she takes a deep, steadying breath, "you know where the door is." Spinning around, not waiting for his reply, Catherine walks over to Ben's office door, then slows, and turns back.

*I thought we were friends. I trusted you!*

"If I was wrong about that..." her voice suddenly loses all its heat, her eyes so full of hurt she would be mortified to see what Ben is so clearly seeing on her beautiful, very pale, face "...maybe I've been wrong about a lot of things." She does leave his office then, her shoulders just a little lower, as if the world and his dog are sitting atop them, and her usually stiff spine, that told the world and his dog not to mess with her, not quite so straight. Not quite so braced to face whatever anyone is stupid enough to throw at her.

Ben sighs deeply, pushing his hands back through his already tousled chestnut hair. It always looks shaggy, he hates going to the barbers, but now it looks positively deranged as he fists two hands full and gives them a mighty squeeze in frustration. Letting out a pained growl, he stalks over to slam the door that Catherine has left open. For a full five minutes he stalks, though that takes some doing in his box of an office, around and around then up and down all the while muttering to himself.

"Try to look out for someone. Try to ease their burden and make life just that little bit easier...," growling now he paces, his hands seemingly throttling an invisible neck "...but no, not for this woman. She has to do every flaming thing herself. Or tries to," he glowers at the door, seeing the image of Catherine as she'd looked before she left.

Turning his face up to the ceiling, asking the powers-that-be for strength, Ben takes in an enormous breath, holds it then dispels it very slowly. Who is he kidding; Catherine has never taken the easy way in anything. He doubts she has ever had the opportunity. When he met her, is it really six years ago, he'd been a twenty-one year old computer sciences major fresh out of university, and she'd been a skinny nineteen year old self taught computer genius just starting to make it big in the world of security systems. And she hadn't been installing other people's security programmes; Ben remembers proudly, she had been writing them herself, customising them to her client's exact needs. Moreover, as yet, they have never been breached.

Smiling, Ben remembers why he puts up with her snarling insults and tumultuous rages. She is as temperamental as any dedicated artist is. And her computer programmes are a work of art he acknowledges, slumping down into his pride and joy of a chair. Whatever happened to Catherine before they met, and he's sure something very bad did happened, it drove her to succeed.

"Time to make a large mug of steaming hot chocolate, me thinks." His smile deepens and reaches his pale grey eyes putting a twinkle in them. Walking to Catherine's office five minutes later, the mug he brought her back from his last trip abroad in hand, Ben knocks on the door and waits..., and waits. About to stalk off, his smile slipping as he calls himself a fool for bothering to make the damned drink, the door finally opens.

Catherine stands looking at him, her shoulders back and her spine ramrod straight, warning him, without the need for words, that she's ready to go another round if that's what he's come for. But he just stands there, his placatory smile back in place, his hand wafting over a mug, her mug she notes, pushing the steam rising out of it in her direction. Then she catches it - the scent of her favourite hot chocolate drink, no doubt made exactly as he knows she likes it. Assailing her olfactory senses it melts her mood away, just as he hoped it would.

*Oh baby, come to momma!*

"Give me that," and snatching the proffered mug right out of his hands, barely manages to avoid scalding them.

"You're welcome, I'm sure," Ben smiles, though still a little tentatively. Moving over to take a seat in front of Catherine's desk, Ben eyes her again, this time with concern as he notes her reddened eyes. "Have you been crying?" he gasps in amazement. "I mean...," Ben is almost stammering "...you never do...I've never seen..." *Shit!*

"And you haven't now," Catherine denies, coughing on a mouthful of very hot chocolate that she had been enjoying a moment before. "So don't you go round saying any different!"

*For god's sakes, where's a mirror when you need one!*

Standing up, eyes darting about, Catherine searches for a mirror she already knows she doesn't own or a handy reflective surface that might at least indicate how bad the problem is. "My bloody eyes are just a bit tired," she defends quickly, "and I'd just been rubbing at them before you came creeping at my door." *Fuck it!* She knows she is being mean, but she will not have him thinking she is weak. Will not let anyone think she is weak.

Catherine has experienced the consequences of weakness, has suffered the vile hands of her first employer grasping and groping all over her young body.

*Oh, shit!*

A hand flies over her mouth to stifle a scream at the unexpected bombardment of a crystal clear memory. She can even smell his foul tobacco breath, stale from a cigarette break he'd taken out back of the shop. The remembered stench fills her nostrils and Catherine flees the office for the next-door loo, Ben's cries of "Are you alright?" barely registering.

Watching her mad dash; not even taking the time to pull the loo door closed after her, Ben listens as Catherine retches into the bowl until she is retching up nothing but air. Hearing water running in the tiny sink, he imagines her splashing it over her face as he listens to the repeated scooping and falling of water. Stepping back into her office, Ben hurriedly retakes his seat, knowing she will feel humiliated if she comes out to find him standing there, witness to her loss of control. He grimaces as he hears her close the door quietly behind him.

*Oh god, now what?*

Rounding her desk and taking her seat, Catherine can't lift her eyes to meet Ben's, knowing what she will see there. "It appears I owe you an apology," she begins, holding up a still trembling hand to stay any response Ben might make. "It seems I'm not as well as I'd thought." *No shit, Sherlock!*

Taking a shaky breath, she taps into her computer and brings up the progress reports for the Kingsley account. The account she is going to have to leave to Ben after all. "Your progress reports show a lot of work still to do."

Slipping firmly back into work mode, Catherine flicks through screens of reports, making brief notes on a jotter to indicate priority areas for completion, and instructions for alterations to others. Handing him the torn off sheet of paper, still not meeting his eyes full on, Catherine stands as she says, "We're due to install the first layer of programming and start the information dissemination process at Kingsley's by the end of the month. That gives us just over two weeks." She almost meets his eyes then, but uses the manoeuvre of picking up her scruffy sack bag as she makes her way out of the office to avoid full eye contact. Even before he could voice a reply, Catherine is gone.

The front door slamming shut behind her gives Ben a jolt. Still sitting in her office, he ponders the recent events. His brows draw together, pulling back the image of Catherine's face just before she bolted from the room.

She had barely seemed to be there. Her mind, if not her body, had been in another place and time he is sure. That blank look followed by her suddenly paling face and darting eyes, told him she was seeing something that he could not. And it worried him. She'd been terrified, he is sure of it. Whatever she had been recalling is what had turned Catherine's stomach.

"Not feeling well," he snorts aloud. "Well, that's as maybe, but that's not what this is all about and we both know it." Walking back to his office, Ben immerses himself deep into his demanding work, pushing all thoughts of Catherine's troubles to the back of his mind, as he's had to do many times in the past.

He has known from the start that she is a troubled soul, has tried to offer support and a listening ear, but she refused both. He just hoped that one day, when she came to trust him enough, she would tell him of her own accord.

## <u>Chapter Two</u>

The beat up old Ford Fiesta that Catherine has been driving since she passed her test at eighteen appears to be heading for that great scrap heap in the sky. *Bloody hell!* "Come on baby, don't do this to me today of all days." Afraid of flooding the engine, but too desperate not to give it yet another try, Catherine turns the engine over again. *Please baby!* With a gasp and a wheeze, the car springs to life and Catherine places a grateful kiss on the steering wheel. "Yes…you beauty!" *Thank Christ for that!*

Turning in her seat, she flips through her folder one last time. "If I've forgotten anything now I'll just have to wing it." But she knows she hasn't, she is far too obsessive to do that. Catherine never gives a second thought to what she looks or sounds like, just as long as her work is first rate and the client gets exactly what they specified. Or worked out together more accurately, Catherine smiles to herself. That's the part she really enjoys – like a jigsaw; it's looking at the parts already in play then designing other parts that enhance the whole and make it complete. Or, worse case scenario, designing a completely new system and the software to get the best out of it.

Pulling into the car park of Kingsley Import & Export Ltd, Catherine secures the paperwork in its folder then hooks her old sack bag over her shoulder. Entering the ultra-modern building through floor to ceiling glass doors, she walks up to the receptionist who watches her approach with a sceptical expression down a nose that could give an Olympic ski slope a run for its money. *Wow.*

"May I help you?" Catherine eyes the receptionist and has to smile, knowing this toffee-nosed bitch would like nothing more than to help her back out the door with a kick up her arse.

*Ok bitch, you wanna play.*

"We haven't met," Catherine thrusts out her hand deliberately, knowing the woman will not want to take it, and she is right. However, professional to the last, the receptionist touches Catherine's fingers as briefly as possible then quickly wipes her own hand on her skirt. "If you wouldn't mind letting Mr Kingsley know that Colson is here, that'd be great," and even throws in a smile. *See, I'm playing nice.*

"But madam...," *Don't you madam me, bitch.* Catherine's eyes narrow at the overbearing woman's tone "...both Mr Kinsley's are very busy men; you can't just walk in off the street and expect them to see you!" *That does it!*

"Off the street...," Catherine repeats quietly, so quietly that it would have set alarm bells ringing in anyone who knew her. However, this woman has never met Catherine before yet she is judging her and finding her wanting in every way. "Yes, I imagine that's where you think I live.*" You trumped up snobby cow.* The receptionist gasps at her frankness. "But I guarantee that's where you'll be taking a long walk after I get through telling Arthur you've made me late for our appointment. Now pick that fucking phone up and tell him that Colson arrived five minutes ago and you're very sorry for making her late for our meeting." *You judgemental bitch!*

Taking a few steps away from the desk to pull her temper in, Catherine does indeed hear the woman apologise to Arthur Kingsley when he confirms that she is due to meet with him this morning.

"If you would take the first lift to the ninth floor Mr Kingsley's PA will escort you to his office." Her manner is stiff and polite, but Catherine enjoys it most when she watches her swallow down on the bile that is no doubt choking her when she adds, "And, I'm very sorry for any misunderstanding, Ms Colson."

*Stick it!*

Not even bothering to reply, Catherine strides over to the lift and makes her way up for her meeting. She hates being late for anything – it's a pet hate; or an obsession if Ben is to be believed.

The woman who greets Catherine on the ninth floor could not be more different. They met on a previous visit, but Diane Waters had been just as welcoming then as she is now. "Colson..." Diane smiles warmly and holds both hands out to take Catherine's, "...how lovely to see you again. Arthur is in the informal meeting room – I hope you don't mind but a family friend, who is also a business associate, has arrived a little earlier than expected. But Logan is such a lovely man, I'm sure there won't be a problem." *Bloody hell!* Diane gives a brief knock then immediately shows Catherine in.

Arthur Kingsley is a very young and spritely sixtyyear-old man with an infectious laugh and a broad grin, and Catherine took to him right off. "Colson, my dear, come on in, come and sit over here by me." Arthur pats the seat of a luxuriously appointed honey beige settee that is like nothing you would ever see in a house. It can easily seat six, and is one of three set at right angles to form three sides of a square, in the centre of which is set a large glass topped table that reminds Catherine of a small lake. Arthur stands as she draws nearer and waits while she takes a seat before retaking his own.

"How are you doing, Arthur?" Catherine asks, making an effort to put her temper aside and concentrate on being professional. It had been difficult to use his Christian name at first, but he had insisted and she'd settled into it quickly, realising that Arthur is a man after her own heart. He doesn't stand on ceremony and doesn't let anyone else.

*A genuine down-to-earth rich bloke - you don't get many of them to the pound!*

"Actually...," he smiles with boyish mischief in his eyes, "...I'm doing rather well. I'm giving it all up and retiring to a life of riley." *What the hell!*

Catherine is mortified on his behalf. "Arthur, you're too young to retire; surely they can't make you go?" Scowling deeply, she imagines 'they' as a bunch of gargoyles sitting around a huge table and who made up the Board that had no doubt told him that he is too old, or too something that they don't approve of.

*Bloody gits!*

But it isn't Arthur that answers. A young man of around thirtyish comes striding over from a corner of the room where she hasn't noticed him having a drink with another man who remains where he is, half hidden in the shadows. "No one's forcing him to leave, Colson," Robert Kingsley smiles broadly, a cup of strong tea in hand. "Logan and I..." he waves a hand over to the man he's been talking to in the far corner of the room, "...have tried to talk the old man into staying on even in a part time capacity but he says he's done enough and it's time for the fun to begin."

Robert casts his father an affectionate look and has it returned ten-fold. "Now...Diane's made up a fine table with tea, coffee, biscuits and muffins; what would you like? – and don't say nothing or we'll all be in trouble," he jokes giving a mock shudder in the direction of Diane's closed adjoining office door.

Catherine accepts a cup of black coffee and a couple of chocolate-chip biscuits, and tries not to peer into the shadows that are hiding the mysterious visitor that Robert is again in conversation with.

*Could be shy. Could be ugly. Or you could just be another arrogant shit who thinks he's too good to mix with such lowly company!*

Logan Sayers has no such reservations. His position in the room gives him the advantage of being able to assess Catherine openly. He's heard both Arthur and Robert address her as Colson, yet he knows her name to be Catherine from an earlier conversation with Robert. Possibly a nickname he muses, taking another sip of his tea. He realises then that Robert is repeating something he's already said and Logan makes more of an effort to pay attention. But it doesn't last; his eyes are drawn inexorably back towards the young woman with the severe haircut and the most unflattering baggy clothes. She is like some sort of stray mongrel, like no woman he's ever met yet knows instinctively that she is more than she appears on the surface. The puzzle is, how much more and why is he so interested in finding out?

As Catherine and Arthur conclude their business, Robert moves across the room to say his goodbye, or so Logan thinks.

"Colson, don't rush off." Robert smiles warmly at Catherine, obviously quite taken by her. "As we were saying earlier, my father is insisting on retiring so we're insisting on giving him a good send off. It'll be at the end of next month and we'd love you to be there, wouldn't we?" He turns an encouraging look on his father, obviously wanting his backing.

"Wouldn't be the same without you," Arthur reiterates enthusiastically, and Catherine knows they both mean it.

*Ok Brain-of-Britain, think of something!*

Catherine hesitates; she really does not go out, as in being social and actually making conversation for the sake of it. She's never seen the point for one thing. "I'm not sure...I don't really think..." *Help!*

However, Robert isn't taking no for an answer. "That's settled then," he states, steamrolling over any further protests. "I can arrange a car to pick you up..." then adds "...and your escort, of course, or a friend of your choosing?" when Catherine still doesn't look convinced.

*Friend! What friend? I don't do friends!*

"Fine..." she finds herself agreeing awkwardly, "...I'll ask Ben if he can make it." *Are you nuts? Socialising? Really?*

"Well that's great," Robert smiles slyly. "And now that you've agreed to go to my father's bash you can hardly miss mine. Wouldn't be fair at all would it...?" *What? I need to get out of here!*

"Yours...I don't understand...what bash?" *I feel faint.* She is starting to flail, feeling totally out of her depth.

"It's my thirtieth birthday in a week's time – though we're having the party the night after rather than the night of," he laughs. "Can't get rat-faced on a Thursday so it's going to have to be on the Friday, and we can make the same transportation arrangement for you and Ben...or whoever you decide to bring?" *Bloody buggering hell!*

"I can get myself to both dos," she tells him, making to leave before he can talk her into anything else.

"So you are coming then." *No! No! No!* Robert laughs at her forlorn frown. "That's great, and I promise you'll have a good time." *Whoopee!*

Catherine eyes him doubtfully then turns to smile at Arthur. "Thanks for your time, Arthur. I have copies of everything so don't feel you have to rush or return the paperwork. But if you've got any queries you know how to reach me." *Now let me out of here!*

"I'm sure it will all be fine," he assures her. "Now go and enjoy the rest of the day. The sun is shining and you could do with a little more colour in your cheeks."

*I'd have more colour in my cheeks if your bloody son would stop cornering me into things I'd really rather not do!*

Turning she acknowledges the stranger with a grimace more than a smile and a very brief nod of her head. *Holy fuck, he's built like He-man and looks like a Norse God — shame he's such a stiff-necked son-of-a-bitch!*

Taking her completely off guard, Logan thrusts his hand forward expectantly waiting for her to shake it. "Ms Colson." *Holy cow!*

Not wanting to appear petulant or ignorant, Catherine takes his hand and feels a jolt of electricity shoot up her arm to addle her brains. *God Almighty – what the hell was that!*

Her bright blue eyes flash up to his face and she knows that he felt it too.

"Mr Sayers." *You know what you're doing to me, don't you?* The only reason she hasn't snatched her hand back is because Logan is holding it in a firm but gentle grip.

After what feels like forever, Logan lets go of her hand and Catherine makes a speedy exit. *Phew!*

Berating herself all the way back to her bedsit – *and yes it is still the same one she moved into at seventeen* - Catherine feels the heat in her cheeks when she remembers how her hand had felt in Logan's and rubs it on her thigh to erase the memory.

However, she can't erase the memory of how Mr high and mighty Sayers had looked at her. *As if she was something he'd wipe off the sole of his fancy shoes, no doubt.*

Well tough shit, she doesn't dress up for anyone, and anyone who expects her to can take a long run off a very short pier. *And drown!*

The night of Robert Kingsley's birthday bash is looming large and Catherine has nothing appropriate to wear. Why would she. All she possesses are a few long baggy jumpers that she wears over equally baggy tracky bottoms. All of them purchased from the local Oxfam shop and somehow, she doesn't see them running to anything that Robert Kingsley's crowd might be wearing this season to a posh do. *Shame.*

For the first time, Catherine enters a fashion boutique. At least, she tries to. One look from the snooty sales clerks has her turning tail before she's put a second foot in the door of one particularly smart shop. But then her loud cry of "Holy fuck," as her eyes lighted on a price ticket for a strikingly plain evening dress might have something to do with it. She'll be more prepared for the next one, she vows.

Staring in the window of another fancy boutique, Catherine decides she just has to get on, do it, and not take any crap from the snobby cows that are no doubt going to earn a whacking great commission at her expense. *And I don't even want to go to the damn party!*

Wiping her damp palms down the sides of her jumper, Catherine enters the lion's den. *I can do this...*

The sales clerk is unexpectedly nice and very helpful, offering advice and suggesting suitable accessories. Feeling that she should at least be honest with someone who is being so nice, Catherine fesses up, "I've never even bought a dress before, or a skirt, come to that." *Why would I?*

"Don't you worry, dear," the sales clerk smiles warmly, "it took me years to get my daughter into a dress – she was very much a tom-boy right up to her late teens." Shaking her head at the memory, the sales clerk guides Catherine over to the changing rooms.

Trying on the dress and the dainty shoes in the small cubicle, the sales clerk stifles a chuckle when she hears a plaintive, "Fuck me," precede the undignified exit of Catherine from one of the cubicles to face the now smiling clerk. *I can't do this...* "How the bloody hell am I supposed to walk in these?" she asks, wobbling dangerously on the impossibly high heels.

Back at the office, she asks Ben if he's sorted his outfit out for the big bash. He'd been both surprised and delighted that she'd thought to invite him as her escort; yet had been secretly staggered at the thought of Catherine accepting an invitation to go anywhere. Let alone a birthday party for one of Britain's richest and most eligible bachelors.

That last thought has given Ben a few twinges, thinking Catherine might actually be attracted to the man, though her response to that suggestion put the lid firmly on any such ideas.

"We'll stay as long as we have to," Catherine scowls at Ben, "and if himself has a mind for anything other than a friendly smile I expect you to deck him!"

Ben laughs at that; then swallows noisily, nervously, foolishly reassuring himself that she doesn't really mean him to take her literally.

Arriving at the party venue, Ben hands the keys to his sports car over to the chap in charge of valet parking. Taking Catherine's elbow, he steers her up the steps to the hotel entrance doors where she stares open mouthed at all the bling on display. "Bloody hell!" Looking down at her midnight blue satin sheath, that falls from shoestring shoulder straps to the matching shoes beneath; Catherine scowls at her unadorned self, then sets her spine straight, holds her head up and keeps her eyes firmly forward.

*I'm every bit as good as you are, I just can't walk in these bloody heels!*

The grand ballroom is bedecked in the kind of lavish trimmings, huge ice sculptures and chocolate fountains that Catherine had never even dreamed of. The envious stares of so many of the female guests pass her by completely.  As do the admiring glances, many of the rich and powerful men are giving her. Only Ben, who quickly reminds her that she has promised to be on her best behaviour, hears her thankfully breathy, stunned exclamation of, "Fuck."

Logan Sayers, however, hasn't missed her entrance. Nor has he missed the expletive she uttered. From across the room he read her unpainted lips as clearly as if she were standing next to him. He watches her, surprised by her grace of movement, though she refuses all offers to dance. Even from Ben, he observes with no small measure of satisfaction.

Then Robert Kingsley sought her out. He refuses to take no for an answer when he asks her to dance, and guides her inexperienced feet expertly round the dance floor. She actually laughs with enjoyment when the dance is over; stating that he must be a seriously good dancer if he can make even her look as if she actually knows what she's doing.

Between the attentions of Ben and Robert Kingsley, Catherine is getting steadily drunk. *So what, it's the weekend and I'm the boss, so there.* Feeling a strong hand take hold of her arm, Catherine turns dizzily to face an angry looking Logan Sayers. "You're drunk," he states drawing her out onto a wide terrace, his ever so haughty aristocratic voice making his observation sound like an accusation.

"Actually, I'm piss-faced," she corrects, mimicking his accent and drawing a reluctant smile to his lips. She finds herself staring at those lips. Has no idea why she so badly wants to taste them. *So full and soft and...* Shaking her head, Catherine tries to pull out of his grip but it doesn't loosen in the slightest. Frowning she looks up, trapped in his gaze, like a startled deer in front of the headlights on a lorry that surely spells its doom. *Heman...Norse God...* Then, as if the lorry really has done its worst, Catherine's world goes black as she passes out.

Back at her bedsit, Logan easily manages to carry Catherine and get the keys to her bedsit out of her evening bag. He pushes the door open and walks into a double sized bedroom that makes up Catherine's entire living area. Switching on the light, he kicks the door closed and makes his way over to her bed.

Bending carefully, Logan pulls back the quilt as he makes to lay Catherine down. But as he does so her arms come around his neck, her nose nuzzling close and her sleepy voice says, "You smell nice." He stiffens, not quite sure how to proceed then smiles down at her. "You smell pretty nice yourself."

He knows she isn't wearing perfume, but the innocent smell of soap and talcum powder is just as alluring. She has a smile playing over her lips and he wonders what she is thinking about. "Catherine, I'm going to have to take this dress off and help you into bed."

"You're...taking me to bed?" Her brow creases, but her eyes don't even open.

"No, Catherine, I'm going to help you get into bed but I need to help you out of this dress first. It'll be ruined if you sleep in it," he states matter-of-fact.

Sliding her down his body to stand on the floor, her wobbly legs barely manage to hold her up. Slipping both straps off her shoulders, he watches the slinky fabric puddle on the floor at her feet. "You really are full of surprises," he whispers softly as he lifts then lays her on the bed. He can't help but admire how well she fills out the lacy bra and how feminine she looks wearing the matching lacy briefs. Pulling the covers up, and tucking them gently in around her, Logan gazes down at one of the most intriguing women he's ever met.

Picking up her evening gown, Logan takes a very short walk around her tiny one room dwelling. He is astounded that she actually manages to live in it; though exist would be a more accurate description, he thinks dryly. But he gives Catherine credit for her housekeeping. There isn't a thing out of place. Then he takes another look around and decides there actually doesn't appear to be much of anything to leave lying around. Not even a single framed photo on display.

Opening the small wardrobe, Logan hangs up the gown, and fingers the meagre amount of clothing that hangs there. Is her business doing so badly, he puzzles, his mind trying to make sense of what little he knows of Catherine Colson? He turns to look at her then. She has rolled herself up tight in her blankets, clutching them to her like a shield. He has seen her almost naked when he removed her evening gown, leaving only her obviously new underwear in place. She is shapelier than he'd imagined, even her evening gown had skimmed over and hidden her secrets well he mused. Yet she looks now like a frightened child. Then as if in response to his thoughts she tosses in her sleep becoming even more entangled in the blankets.

Logan finds himself sitting on the edge of the bed and leaning over to stroke what little there is of her silky soft hair. A small murmur, a word he can't make out, is spoken into the night, and a single tear spills down her cheek as she turns her still sleeping face towards him.

"Bloody cheek!" Catherine screws up the note that Logan has left, advising her not to drink, as alcohol obviously does not agree with her, then cradles her throbbing head. *Never again!* What the fuck had she been drinking anyway? She frowns down into the strong black coffee that is all she's having for breakfast. Just the thought of food is enough to make her stomach roil.

Then a thought finally strikes her. Unthinkingly she had reached for her dressing gown on waking, pulling it tight around herself as she padded around the room in a groggy stupor. Now that the strong black coffee is kicking in, her thoughts have begun to clear. How had she gotten to bed after the party? Indeed, how had she gotten home? Had Ben brought her home? Had he undressed her and put her to bed. She groans with embarrassment, and then remembers the note.

How the hell had Logan Sayers managed to leave her a note on the top of her computer? Had he come back with her and Ben? Had he been in the room when Ben had undressed and put her to bed? Please God, no. Feeling almost faint at the thought, she asks herself the question she has been avoiding. Or had it been Logan Sayers alone who had brought her home, had taken off her clothes before putting her to bed like a drunken teenager? She pulls open her dressing gown; looking down at the scraps of lace the sales clerk had laughingly called underwear.

*Holy shit!* With an audible gasp, she draws the dressing gown even more tightly around her. "He's near as damn it seen me naked," she moans aloud. "I don't even know the man and he's seen me naked!" Catherine's embarrassment is fast turning to anger. What the bloody hell was Ben doing while Logan Sayers was apparently doing just as he damned well pleased? *Naked!*

The long shower and the slow uneventful drive to work have done nothing to improve Catherine's mood. Striding into the office she begins tearing a strip off the still suffering Ben. "What the bloody hell happened last night?" Catherine shouts then has to turn the volume down as she's making her own head throb. *Either that or the Numbskulls are playing the sodding bongos.* The fact that Ben is obviously suffering too does nothing to soften her tone.

"I asked you to escort me on one of the very rare occasions that I allow myself to get bulldozed into being sociable – and what do you do...you fucking brain dead moron...you let me get hammered! Plastered! Fucking piss-faced!" She groans then and crumples onto a chair. "And who the bloody hell got me home and into bed?" *Not Logan. Not Logan. Oh God!* Her voice may have softened but her blue eyes, though narrowed, were giving off sparks.

Ben looks up then, his brows drawn together deep in thought. "Well I sort of assumed that, as Robert had offered me the use of a guest room, one of many they booked for just such an emergency, he'd made you the same offer. But...obviously not," he finishes lamely then shoves two Aspirin into his mouth and gulps down a glass of water.

"You've got no idea have you?" Catherine accuses. "I could have been abducted by Jack-the-bloody-Ripper for all you cared." *Raped! Murdered!*

"Now don't let's get this all out of proportion," Ben tries to reason. "I mean...it's not like Robert or his father would have invited anyone with a dodgy character, is it?" He asks hopefully.

"They invited you didn't they?" But they hadn't she realises, she had. Then she hears her telephone ringing and makes her way reluctantly into her own office. "God almighty!" She grimaces, lunging for the phone just to stop the insane noise. "What?"

"Well, I don't have to ask how your head is this morning." It's Logan Sayers and she can just imagine the superior smile that would be on his smug face.

About to say something scathing, Catherine remembers that he must have been the one who had gotten her home safe, if not sound. *Naked! Oh Lord.* "I suppose you want me to thank you?" she asks ungraciously.

"On the contrary...I don't want or expect anything from you." The fact that he sounds sincere only serves to aggravate Catherine even more.

"I didn't ask you to take me home, you know," she states and can hear the childish petulance in her own voice.

"You didn't ask me to tuck you up in bed either," and she can definitely hear the smile in his voice now, "but I did."

Her cheeks flame and so, naturally for her, does her temper. "Well you don't have to sound so fucking righteous and pleased about it." *Jesus!* Catherine hears a rumbling chuckle and continues hotly, "I don't suppose you know anything about enjoying yourself. You were probably drinking cups of bloody tea all night." *I wish I had.*

"I'll just have to prove you wrong about that," Logan challenges.

"About what?" she asks, feeling suddenly confused. *The Numbskulls are still playing the damned bongos in her head!*

"About the fact that I do indeed know how to enjoy myself," he states pleasantly; then adds, "I just prefer a good game of rugby to getting drunk for enjoyment."

"I...I..." She gives up. Catherine doesn't have a clue what to say to that.

"Lost for words, hey – that must be a first." He is chuckling again, but stops when he hears her low growl. "Well, I think as payment for seeing you safely home last night the least you can do is to come and support my team tomorrow."

Catherine remains silent for half a minute and Logan finds himself nervously awaiting her answer.

"You want me to stand on some park side-line, no doubt freezing my arse off, while you run around with a bunch of other hunks cradling, throwing and generally trying to put a ball, which isn't even a proper ball, over some bloody line?" she summarises with no little sarcasm.

*As if!*

"You've got it exactly," he announces with another chuckle. "But, according to the weather men, you won't be freezing your lovely arse off, it's supposed to be sunny and warm all day."

"Will you stop with the lovely arse comment!" she growls out quietly so that Ben won't hear, "It's not like I invited you in, and you know it."

Laughing openly and loud, not quite sure why he is feeling so pleased with himself, he makes an effort to placate her. "You are absolutely right, and I promise to behave more like a gentleman if you promise to come to the game tomorrow. I'll even pick you up," he offers.

"You bet your arse you will," she capitulates ungraciously.

"That's a date then," he confirms before Catherine has time to change her mind, "I'll pick you up at nine thirty."

*A date – who said anything about a bloody date!*

Left holding the receiver with no one on the other end, Catherine gives it a good glare and slams it down, then grimaces as her head pounds painfully.

Logan leans back in his chair with a foolish grin on his face. She called him a hunk; he congratulates himself, conveniently ignoring the fact that she had lumped him in with the rest of the team. He stands, all six feet four of him, broad muscular shoulders rippling as he gives his impressive body a good stretch while walking over to look out of his office window. It's raining and overcast; but to Logan it is a lovely sunny day.

As they pull into the club car park next morning, Logan explains the procedure. "I need to go to the changing room, which is strictly men only I'm afraid," he teases, and actually receives a reluctant smile from Catherine, "but you can get a coffee in the club house while you're waiting. I've already told Mary to expect you; the wives organise the food and drink on a rota basis they sort out between themselves." He got out and rounded the car to open her door but Catherine has already climbed out by the time he reaches her.

She catches her breath at his sudden nearness and inhales him deeply. Damn, what a body. Managing to stop the sudden impulse to reach out and explore that lovely expanse of chest right in front of her, Catherine gulps audibly.

"Catherine...?" Logan asks when she doesn't speak.

Thoroughly annoyed with herself she turns a flushed grimace up at him. "I wish you wouldn't call me that...it's a sissy name and I don't like it. Everyone else just calls me Colson." *But you are definitely not like everyone else...*

"I refuse to call any lady by her surname, it's rude," he states in his best Etonian voice. "And I like Catherine, it's a lovely English name that reminds me of tea roses and lilac, bluebells and snowdrops." He reaches a large, very gentle hand up to run his fingers down her pale cheeks.

"You have alabaster skin, so smooth and pale." His touch makes her breath catch and her heart flutter wildly, and when his thumb brushes over her sensitive lips, she feels it right down where her panties are growing wet and groans audibly. "What a contradiction of images you present. So full of fire and steel one moment then so warm and sensual the next." He doesn't finish his thoughts as they have taken a very erotic turn. Instead, he drops his hand and moves to the boot of the car to get his kit bag.

*No...come back...don't leave me like this...*

Catherine has not moved or spoken a word, just that one groan of pleasure that she hadn't been able to stifle. Her heart is still fluttering then jumps wildly when he calls over, pulling her abruptly out of her stunned reverie.

"We'd better make a move." He indicates the other cars parked nearby. "Looks like most of the team are already here and I need to get changed," he smiles broadly.

The game is awesome. Considering the size of the players, they are fast on their feet and lithe of movement. Catherine finds herself cringing and worrying for Logan's well-being during some of the fierce tackles and scrums that are played; but, she gives him his due, he's giving as good as he gets and usually comes out on top. She even finds herself cheering him on; then giving a player on the opposing team a piece of her mind when she feels he's made a dirty tackle on Logan who, minutes later, goes on to score the first try of the match.

In the clubhouse later, the rowdy teams are enjoying a pint and a good-natured dig at each other over various plays they had made or missed.

A young buck from the opposing team tries to impress Catherine, asking her why she is wasting her time with the old has-beens and invites her to join his group, who are standing behind him looking hopeful.

Catherine, however, is far from impressed. Talking loud enough for the 'has-beens' to hear, Catherine looks up at the twenty-something player and says, "One particular so called has-been ran rings around you to score the first try of the match." To a cheer from the men at the bar, Catherine continues, "And the rest of them very nearly whipped your sorry arse. You won by a drop kick and a lucky breeze," she smiles witheringly, "now go finish your beer like a good little boy." Turning back to the bar, she raises a celebratory pint of shandy, as ordered by Logan, for an excellent match that was only lost by a last minute drop-kick that was on the dodgy side in her lowly opinion.

## Chapter Three

Logan is distracted and uncharacteristically snappy during the following week. He hasn't found an excuse to contact Catherine, he refuses to think of her as Colson, and has been thinking about her entirely too much.

He knows she is tied up with the preparations for implementing the first phase of the Kingsley deal; knows, too, that she has been worried about her lack of input during the final stages of putting the software package together.

A wistful smile tips up his lips. He had invited Catherine home for Sunday lunch after the rugby match last week, and she had happily accepted. Mrs Baines was her usual adaptable self and had made Catherine feel at ease about the impromptu invitation. They'd had lunch in the conservatory with a bottle of white wine and the conversation between them had never stopped.

The afternoon had turned to evening before either of them realised, they were talking and laughing like old friends. Catherine's business with Arthur and Robert was apparently going well, though she had expressed some concerns about it, Catherine hadn't gone into detail. Mostly they had discussed the rugby match and the cheeky youngster from the opposing team – he'd been particularly pleased when she'd dismissed him out of hand. Sure, Catherine had been shy at times, Logan remembers her pink cheeks and coy smile, but for the most part they had talked comfortably and enjoyably until midnight.

She needs a break, he decides, remembering the stress on Catherine's face when she had talked about her workload and the expanding business. Then he thinks of Lakelands, a small estate where he grew up and where his father still lives.

Yes, he will convince her to go for a couple of days, he decides; then realises he is actually nervous at the thought. He laughs at himself, having never been nervous around women. Indeed, he finds them a source of great pleasure, both in and out of bed. He treats women with great respect, his own pleasure heightened by the simple act of tending to his companions needs first.

Catherine, he realises, is an entirely different prospect. She manages to throw him off balance. Seems to be a contradiction of personalities all tied up in that Colson persona that she clings to; but who is he attracted to, Catherine or Colson?

Catherine has also been distracted at work; only her reaction to the unwelcome intrusion of a personal life is an even more aggressive immersion in to her work.

Ben is ducking for cover. Catherine is stomping around like a bear with a sore head, and her language would redden even the most seasoned ears.

"The Bastard!" he hears Catherine shriek, just after hearing her telephone slam down in its cradle. Then Ben listens to the sound of her stomping the short distance to his office. "That bloody Bastard, Davis!" Catherine storms, shaking with temper as she stands in Ben's doorway. "He's just cancelled. The fucking jumped up, smarmy excuse for a human being just fucking cancelled!" *What a dick!*

Chesney Davis is a stocky little man who stands about five feet six tall. Catherine knew from their first meeting that he didn't like her one bit, any more than she liked him. He had looked her up and down while remaining seated at the head of a long table surrounded by empty chairs. The boardroom, she had guessed, also guessing that he was trying to impress upon her how important he is. They discussed the outline of a plan to overhaul the current computer system, its security, and the security of the entire company. Catherine had even paid a second visit, putting aside her own feelings, deciding to be professional and get the job done.

The plans she'd drawn up had taken a considerable amount of her valuable time – time she could have spent on the Kingsley account. Now the miserable little man has suddenly cancelled on her. Well, she would bill him for every second that she has wasted on the pillock.

Halfway through her tirade, Catherine hears her telephone ringing. "If that's Davis ringing to change his fucking mind I'll crawl down the line and cut his balls off," she rages, making for her office. "That's if the dickwad even has any!"

Slam. Door closed. The red haze of her anger still visible in his doorway – Ben lets out a relieved breath. *And squeezes his legs together as his balls shrivel up in fear.*

Glaring at the phone, pacing in front of it, Catherine deliberately makes him wait; then snatches it up, hand gripping the receiver so tightly it should have crumpled to dust. "What!" she explodes without preamble. Then deflates like a burst balloon, crumpling into her seat as her misdirected anger gives way to reluctant joy.

"Well," Logan's low chuckle does nothing to improve her mood, "I seem to have caught you at a bad time. Would you like me to call back later?"

She can hear the smile in his voice and it irritates her. "Please yourself."

"Fine, I will," and Logan puts the phone down on her.

Now Catherine is stunned as well as angry. Why the bloody hell did he call in the first place? She had been hoping he would all week, hence her bad mood, but Catherine had given up as the days had passed with no word from Logan.

She spends the next few minutes pacing her office again then decides to call him back. Finding herself put straight through to him, Catherine realises he's been expecting her call. *A bit bloody sure of yourself!*

"Hello, Catherine, how nice to hear from you," he greets her politely.

"Damn it," she exclaims quietly. "Sorry. Ok, I said it, I'm sorry. Now, what did you want?"

He doesn't reply for a minute then says, "How about coming over to my office for lunch?"

Surprising herself, and him, she accepts. Why the hell not. "I can be there in thirty, if that's ok?"

"That's fine...see you soon."

When she arrives in his office, Catherine is still frowning. "What's wrong, Catherine, you look troubled?"

She shrugs, "It's just work, I guess." *That and the time wasting bastard who made me feel like an ugly insect that he wanted to squash!*

After ringing his PA to place the lunch order, Logan sits back in his chair to study Catherine. "It's not the Kingsley deal surely; I thought that was running smoothly?" Logan moves around his desk to sit on the edge of it in front of her. *Holy heck!*

"No, not really, Ben's more than capable of wrapping it up from here." He hasn't heard her sound so dejected before.

"Then what...? You can talk to me about anything, Catherine, you know that, right?"

She jumps up then and stomps around his office, needing to burn off some of the rage that still flames hotly inside her. After telling him the background of the Chesney Davis fiasco, she turns hurt eyes directly on his. "What the fuck do people like Davis want?" She asks, throwing her hands up in the air. "I'm considered brilliant in my field," she exclaims without a hint of arrogance, "so why isn't that enough, damn it?" He can see the baffled hurt in her eyes as she flops back down in her seat. "Why isn't that enough?" she repeats, her voice unexpectedly soft with utter confusion.

There is a war waging in her head and Logan can see it playing out on her lovely face. Yet he has the feeling that the 'pillock' Davis is not the real root of Catherine's problems.

Logan talks about the conventions of business, the expectations that a prospective client might have. "Appearance can exude confidence which is a good portion of what the client is buying. After all they are putting their company into your very capable hands."

"But I'm not comfortable in girl clothes," she states simply. *And no-one can make me wear them!*

Interpreting that to mean that she is not comfortable being looked at as an attractive female and deliberately dresses down to hide her attributes, Logan decides that blunt and honest is the way to go. "Whether you like it or not, Catherine, you are a very attractive, beautiful woman and the baggy clothes and short cropped hair can't hide that fact." *Oh!*

Stunned, Catherine puts a nervous hand to her hair.

*Really?* "You think I'm beautiful?" She asks guilelessly.

Pulling her gently up to her feet, Logan allows his eyes to roam over Catherine hungrily, picturing the lush body that he has seen in all its virtually naked glory. His eyes finally meet hers, noting the deep blush, and realises that she is remembering that he's seen her that way, too.

"I want to kiss you, Catherine?" He is asking her permission she knows, but doesn't realise that he can see the dark shadows of fear so clearly in her eyes.

*Heart racing, hands trembling, her need for him is terrifying.*

Her only reply is an almost imperceptible nod.

Logan's lips hover so close to her own; the heat of his breath causing her lips to tingle expectantly. Just the scent of him, so close, is driving her crazy. Then it is she who closes the gap between them, crushing her lips to his, throwing her arms around his neck to hold him fast while she tastes, nips and sinks willingly into the kiss.

*What is this heat, this need to be held by him? Her thighs press tightly together, trying to stem the uncomfortable surge of longing that has taken her so completely by surprise.*

He plunders her mouth as no man ever has before. Drives her mind to think of wanting things she has only ever found abhorrent; actually wanting him to put his hands on her. Desperately she needs him to fill her, in a way that makes her press into him so intimately that she cannot help but notice how badly he wants her, too. *Holy shit – did I cause that!*

This reality is enough to bring her back from the edge of insanity. Catherine abruptly tears out of his arms and puts some distance between them. He is panting as heavily as she, is holding himself together just as precariously.

*Oh my Lord!*

"I'm sorry," she stammers in a shaky whisper. "I didn't mean..." Her hands lift and fall in a helpless gesture towards him. *Bloody buggering hell!*

"Don't, Catherine, it is my fault entirely. I'm old enough to behave better than that...I'm the one who should apologise." Moving back behind his desk to compose himself, Logan sits down heavily. His loss of control has been as shocking to him as it has evidently been to her. "I didn't mean to frighten you like that," his voice is now soft and comforting. He indicates the chair across from him, "Please, sit down. I promise you, you're quite safe," and smiles to reinforce his declaration.

After taking her seat Catherine stares at her hands in her lap, then quietly takes what for her is a huge leap of faith. *I can't believe I'm going to do this.* "I'm a virgin," she blurts out bluntly. "The only experience I've ever had with men wasn't what anyone would call gentle or romantic." She would have stood, longed to pace about, to grind the memory of her old boss and her mother's death into the luxurious carpet, but isn't at all sure that her legs can support her. *Why are they trembling so badly and why isn't the throb between her thighs going away?* Instead she sits, just waiting for his condemnation of her teasing behaviour; egging him on one minute only to pull away when he began taking her up on her blatant offer the next. *Way to go, Colson!*

Logan is too busy berating himself to start on Catherine. He stares across his desk to the carpet where they had stood. Could envisage himself taking her right there; greedily tearing her clothes off to get at the soft curves of the beautiful body he knows is hidden beneath them. What a gift he marvels, one that he had so very nearly taken without the gentleness and care that such a gift demands.

A brisk knock on the office door announces the arrival of their lunch. Logan's PA serves it with quiet efficiency, and after establishing that they do not require anything else just now, she just as quietly leaves the room.

"I want you to come to Lakelands with me," Logan tells her, making more of a statement than posing an invitation. "It's a small holding in the shires of Branting, just south of the Midlands," he explains, then waits for her response, not realising that he is holding his breath.

"I'd really like to but there's Ben to think of," Catherine replies.

If she had punched him in the gut, she could not have felled him more thoroughly. Indeed, his held breath comes out in a deflating whoosh. "What...?" he asks almost angrily. But Catherine is quick to realise her mistake. *Fuck!*

"No, no..." she holds up a hand of peace, "...I don't mean like that," she assures him. "It's just the Kingsley account; it's coming to a head now and I don't want to just dump it all on Ben's shoulders. It wouldn't be fair," she offers, holding her hands palms up in the air in an expression of helplessness. Then presses nervously on when Logan doesn't make any attempt to reply. "And then there are the new accounts waiting to be evaluated. I can't just drop everything and take off for a few days," she appeals, realising that she is almost pleading with him. *Be reasonable.*

"There will always be new contracts, Catherine. But I think you need to take some time for yourself just now." He smiles winningly. "And anyway, I thought you held Ben's tech skills in high regard?"

*Tricky. Tricky.*

"I do...," she confirms hesitantly, knowing that he is neatly boxing her in.

*You know you want to go so why procrastinate.*

"That's fine then," he concludes with enthusiastic gusto. "If you've finished eating, let's go," and he steers her out of his office, gives a smiling nod to his secretary who is obviously in on his plans, then urges Catherine to step into his private lift.

"Logan..." she begins, but he silences her with a kiss.

This time he is gentle, showing her the pleasure without the fear. His tongue still invades, sending shivers down her spine, but there is none of the frenzy of earlier. By the time they reach the underground car park, Catherine is gloriously breathless, while Logan looks very self-satisfied.

*Who would have thought...that is...mmm.*

"Logan, we can't just take off this minute," she exclaims; but is laughing at the prospect of doing just that. "I don't have any clothes, and neither do you," she giggles, feeling suddenly reckless and carefree.

"Right on the first count," he corrects, also smiling broadly. "I have a wardrobe full of clothes at my father's house, so no problem there. And, by the time we've finished shopping, you won't be short of clothes either."
*Shit, not bloody shopping!*

The boutique that Logan takes her to steals Catherine's breath away. The designs are gorgeous but when she makes a b-line for the trousers section Logan steers her firmly away. "Today is about all things feminine," he tells her, giving a conspiratorial smile to the sales clerk. He walks her round the shop, pulling out dresses, skirts and tops for her to try on. The sales clerk follows on behind, smiling and nodding her approval at his taste, and carrying some of the items when Logan's arms are full.

"Will you stop!" *Are you crazy or what?* Catherine laughs when she eyes the growing pile of clothes she is expected to try on. "If we are really going to your father's today, we don't have time for me to try on the whole of the stock." *I'm only going to look an idiot in them anyway.*

"We are going to my father's today and we will make time for you to try on everything that we've picked out," he says firmly, not giving her any room for excuses.

*Bloody hell!*

The sales clerk hangs all the clothes on a rack in the changing area, passing them through one outfit at a time. "Holy shit!" Catherine's shocked exclamation rings the length of the changing rooms; Logan just smiles winningly at the sales woman. "I imagine she just saw the price tag. Better cover your ears when she gets to the blue dress and jacket, her language will no doubt match the colour." He is chuckling deeply as he says it.

The sales woman has heard it all before, of course. Many women balk at the prices, but all appreciate the quality and style of the exclusive designs.

Logan insists on seeing Catherine in each of the outfits with shoes to match – nodding and smiling his approval and encouragement when she needs it, or shaking his head when something doesn't suit. And she blushes crimson when Logan tries to pick out underwear; whispering to the sales clerk, Catherine gives the woman her cup size and her usual size in panties, then tells her to pack five sets in different colours and no she won't be trying them on, thank you very much.

"Spoil-sport," Logan jokes when he overhears the last part. *Perve!* Then he takes out a credit card from his wallet and makes to pay the bill.

*Well fuck a duck; he thinks he can buy me!*

"What the fuck do you think you're doing?" Catherine asks, staggered that he actually thinks she will let him pay. "I'm not some floozy you just picked up; I can pay for my own clothes, thank you," then thrusts her own card at the sales clerk who is looking from one to the other not wanting to offend either of them.

"Calm down, will you," he placates softly. "I just wanted to treat you. After all, the shopping trip was my idea and I enjoy buying things for my friends; what's the point of having money if you can't enjoy spending it?" he cajoles.

*Just don't get any funny ideas, matey!*

She hesitates. Catherine can see that he is being earnest, but cannot take such an elaborate gift. "Ok..." she concedes reluctantly "...we'll go halves, and that's my final word." *Too damn right!*

He laughs uproariously. "You do know, most women would snap a man's hand off when he offers to buy her a whole new wardrobe of clothes? But then you're not most women, are you Catherine?" He gently cups her crimson cheek and drops a kiss on her forehead.

The sales clerk finishes the transaction, giving Catherine a smile and a nod of respect that both surprises and delights her.

The drive to Lakelands is swift, making best use of the motorways and the comfortable speed of Logan's car. "About another half hour should see us there," he grins at Catherine.

She turns to look at him. He has a relaxed smile on his face that reaches up into eyes full of love. Love for his father, She wonders? Or perhaps it is a love of Lakelands, a feeling of coming home? "You look so content," she ventures softly. "Does going to Lakelands still feel like going home?"

*I can hardly remember what home and family feels like. Will I ever know?*

Turning soft, chocolate brown eyes to look at her, Logan's smile deepens. "You are very intuitive...," he reaches out to cover her hand with his, "...and correct. It has a restorative effect on me. I always come away feeling like a part of Lakelands comes with me, enough to maintain me until the next time I need to come home." Giving her hand a squeeze, he moves his back to the steering wheel as the road narrows and winds hazardously.

"How lovely." Her voice is wistful, dreamy. "All that space, all that room to breathe in the tranquillity of your own little piece of paradise."

Even in the dim light of late evening, Catherine can appreciate the beauty of the countryside. Stone built walls, crafted by skilled hands, are still standing after tens, or maybe even hundreds of years. Hedgerows standing neat and tall provide homes for wildlife and form windbreakers across the fields. She watches as a large grey horse rears up at something she can't see or hear, then gallops off with mane and tail flying.

Oh, to be a horse. The freedom. The speed. *The knackers' yard!*

Logan doesn't speak, not wanting to break the spell, until he knows that Lakelands is coming into view. Turning a wide bend in the road, Logan smiles broadly.

"There she is," he points in front and off to the left.

The evening sky is now red and gold, the sun spilling its last rays over the waters of Lakelands. The many windows glitter like jewels, and the house, which is almost a mansion, stands regal and all alone.

"Oh, Logan," she can't say anymore, the sheer beauty has stolen all her words away. *Beautiful. Just beautiful.*

They drive the rest of the way in quiet anticipation.

Hearing their car door slam, Logan's father, Henry, opens the front door to greet them.

As tall as his son, Henry claps Logan on his back then turns a welcoming smile on Catherine. "Do you have any luggage?" Henry moves towards the boot of the car preparing to carry a suitcase or two, but when the boot pops, he gets an eyeful of the shopping bags and clothing still on their hangers with polythene covers. Raising curious eyebrows over at Catherine, Henry can't help but notice the colour rising in her cheeks.

"It's his fault," she points accusingly at Logan. "The man wouldn't take no for an answer – just kept piling things on until I all but bought the whole bloody shop!" Catherine looks aggrieved and embarrassed, then flushes even deeper when both men turn to face each other and laugh uproariously.

"Don't you worry," Henry tells her, his old brown eyes still glittering with laughter, "his mother was just the same. Ellie didn't compromise on anything, if she couldn't make her mind up between a blue dress and a red suit she'd just buy them both. It seems Logan enjoys shopping, too." *Tell me about it!*

Between them, all the shopping bags, boxes and hangers find their way up to a bedroom that Henry has had made up for Catherine. "You make yourself comfortable," Henry turns to leave, "I've already got supper cooking. Just come down when you're ready – it's nothing that will spoil."

Logan has gone to put the car away and Catherine is glad of some time alone. The bedroom is simply, but beautifully furnished. Admiring the deep bronze curtains that hang at the French windows, Catherine looks out on a balcony. She imagines it would be the perfect place to curl up with a book on a warm evening. Turning to the double bed, she trails her fingers over the beautiful patchwork quilt. Such a skilful blending of so many autumnal colours, with pillows and decorative cushions to match; Catherine can only assume that Henry has a housekeeper, or someone who comes in to help with the house. She definitely cannot see her very masculine host picking out matching cushions, curtains and other soft furnishings. Walking over to a large wardrobe, her toes now scrunching deeply into beige carpet that feels soft enough to sleep on, Catherine begins the tedious job of hanging up her new clothes and putting all the other items away.

Inhaling deeply and exhaling slowly a couple of times helps to steady Catherine's erratic heartbeat and calms her nerves. "He seems nice," Catherine tells herself as she closes the bedroom door, making her way to the staircase, "not too scary, anyway…"

"Not scary at all," Logan interjects behind her then has to shoot out a hand to steady Catherine as she span around, almost toppling off the top step.

"Holy shit!" Hand grasping her now furiously beating heart, her lungs desperately trying to recapture the breath that has been scared out of her, Catherine turns huge blue, startled eyes on Logan. *What the fuck!* "I'm sorry," he manages, trying heroically but failing to stifle a laugh that has his whole body shaking with it.

"You...you...," fighting to free herself from his firm grip, Catherine very nearly topples them both down the staircase, "get off me...get off me, you oaf!"

Realising that Catherine is genuinely upset, Logan sobers quickly. "Catherine, stop – just stop!" he orders gently, but as her arms still fight for freedom, he does the only thing he can think of. He pulls her roughly to him, traps her arms with his and steals all her protests with a kiss.

The moment their mouths meet, she is lost. *His scent. His taste. Him.*

She stills immediately. Instead of the fight or flight response, her body is now responding to something just as primal, just as compelling, and with just the same degree of passion. His lips, gentle at first, have opened to the forceful demand of her tongue. She tastes him now, searching for and giving everything to the kiss. Her arms are now free and her hands reach up and fist in the back of his hair; he isn't close enough, not deep enough, not...not...

His head exploding, his loins burning, Logan manages to break away. "If we don't stop now I'm afraid I won't be able to." He is visibly trembling, and Catherine feels a liberating sense of power to think that she can make this man mountain quiver with need.

"Who says we have to?" She holds his puzzled gaze for a long moment. "I trust you." In that single moment, having uttered the words, Catherine knows them to be true. Right from that first meeting when their hands had touched and a jolt of electricity had passed between them, she had known he was a danger to her equilibrium.

And she had been afraid. But no longer.

It is a simple declaration that is almost his undoing. "You don't know what you're saying." He tries to put even some small distance between them, but Catherine just closes it again. "Catherine, please...I'm not a saint..."

Her smile is dangerous and determined. "Neither am I." Reaching up she slowly pulls his head down, her eyes never leaving his even when their mouths meet. Catherine watches his brown eyes melt, then fire with his growing need. Pressing her aching body into him, she feels the hardness of that need, but this time she isn't afraid. "Let me take you to bed, Logan?"

Her whispered words are an invitation that he cannot resist. "Are you sure?" She nods and smiles, but Logan searches her face before swinging her up into his arms. Striding to her bedroom, he closes the door behind them before he dares take another breath. He wants her so badly, but he has to go slowly. Not only doesn't he want to frighten her, he wants to give her as much of a gift as she is offering him. He will be so gentle; will give her the tenderness that no one else has.

Lifting her jumper over her head, Logan gazes on the youthful beauty that is Catherine. "If you want me to stop, at any time, I promise you I will." It is a promise he knows he will keep, whatever the cost to his sanity. His lips gently touch and his tongue teases against her mouth. Then he begins a slow exploration of her face, her ears, and her lovely neck. *Oh my.*

Catherine's head is spinning, her body pleading for something she doesn't understand. Her nipples are now so hard, all but pushing through the cotton of her bra. And she can feel the wetness of her panties. If she doesn't get naked soon her clothes will surely combust.

Her hands find the elasticated waistband of her tracky bottoms; her thumbs hook inside and begin to tug them down, but Logan stops her. "There's no rush, Catherine. Let me pleasure you and take you to places you never dreamed of." He unfastens her bra, letting it fall to the floor then tastes her until her breath comes in gasping gulps and her fingers dig into his shoulders. Her legs are trembling so badly that he lifts her onto the bed to save her falling. Looking down at her, he can see the plea in her eyes. Logan knows she has no idea what she is pleading for, but he will show her, will allow her the time to experience and explore those needs fully.

He did take off her trousers then and, standing at the foot of the bed gazing down at the miracle of her, removes his own clothing to give her the chance to see him naked. He hears a gasp escape her lips. "I won't hurt you, Catherine," he reassures her softly, "and you can say no at any time."

She watches as he kneels on the bed at her feet then quivers hotly as he opens her legs to move between them. Her panties are still on, but when he lowers his head to taste her through them, she lets out an involuntary scream of pleasure. His gentle hands move under her bottom, sliding beneath her pants to cup her buttocks.

Arching her back off the bed, Catherine's head thrashes side to side as his tongue, teeth and lips graze, bite and tease her mercilessly, while his knowing hands knead her buttocks. "Please...," she screams.

His thumb pulls her cotton pants to one side and the next scream Catherine gives is in shock as much as for the pleasure that tears through her. His tongue is inside her now, finding every sensitive nerve ending, sending her body into the blissful spasms of her first orgasm. Before she has fully come down, he replaces his tongue with expert fingers and his mouth finds her breasts. He takes her back up, her fingers grasping at the bedding trying to stay her, but he makes her fly. "Let go, Catherine." Logan takes her lips and his tongue plunders her mouth as his fingers plunder the growing heat of her sex.

Then her mind and body explode and her world goes instantly black.

When she wakes, Catherine finds Logan smoothing a cold flannel over her brow, smiling. "You fainted," he answers Catherine's unspoken question. Her brows furrow and her eyes search his face for clues. *I've never fainted.*

"Fainted!" Catherine shoots up, almost knocking heads with Logan. "What do you mean, I fainted?" She is panicking now; there must be something wrong with her. "That's not normal, is it?"

His smile widens. "In the old days it was called swooning," he tells her, then gives her a gentle push back on to the pillows. "Do you remember how you felt before you fainted?" *You mean the bit where your tongue was inside me, or the whole imploding thing.*

Catherine certainly does, and a rush of colour stains her otherwise pale cheeks. "I'm not sure," she murmurs, lowering her eyes to the fingers now twisting in the quilt.

"Mmm...," he smiles wickedly, "...perhaps I should refresh your memory," *What!*

Catherine ducks out from under him, grabbing at the sheet that is mostly on the floor pulling it around her. "You promised," she shrieks when Logan makes a playful lunge at her.

He sits up then, shaking his head ruefully. "Me and my big mouth."

She looks at him then, uncertain and shy. "I did it again...I didn't mean to." She feels miserable and confused. *Now he'll think you're a real prick-tease!*

"You did nothing wrong," he tells her softly, all the banter gone from his voice. "Come and sit with me." He holds his hand out toward her encouragingly. "Keep the sheet around you if it makes you feel more comfortable; but I promise I won't touch you like that again until you're ready – and definitely not tonight." *Oh.*

She does keep the sheet around her but not because she doesn't trust him. "I know you wouldn't do anything I didn't want...," Logan moves to sit up; leaning against the headboard he lets her fit herself comfortably against him, "...and, believe me, I have no idea why it all went wrong." She turns her face into his shoulder and kisses him there. "I wanted...no, I want you so badly – I never dreamed I would ever want anyone that way." Catherine pulls his arm tight around her, needing the strength and safety she knows she will find there. *Oh, Logan, if you only knew.*

Enjoying the feeling of her snuggled into him, Logan kisses the top of her head. "By 'that way' do you mean the overwhelming response you experienced, or that you didn't think you would ever want sex?" He knows she is blushing, he can feel the heat of her cheek against his chest.

"Both, I think." *Bloody hell.* She tries to sort her thoughts and feelings out, but her body is still throbbing in a strangely exciting but scary way, and her thoughts are mixing with horrific memories from her past; a past Logan knows nothing about. "The only man to touch me before you was my first employer when I was seventeen." Taking a deep cleansing breath, she decides that this is the least she can tell him. "I had only been out of foster care for a few weeks. My social worker helped me to find the bedsit and the job – I was in seventh heaven. Free, at last, in a home I didn't have to share with anyone else." Catherine looks up at Logan, her blue eyes glinting with remembered excitement. "I could just be me; for the first time ever, including the time I had with my mum, I could do and be anything I chose with no one there to judge me or call me a freak." *Just me, myself and I. The best friends I ever had.*

Logan puts a hand to her cheek, his thumb gently caressing it. "You're not a freak and you never were," he assures her. "I'm glad you were finally happy, but what happened to change that?"

"Mr Shipley happened," Catherine lowers her head and her eyes, but not before Logan sees the clouds gather in them. "He was the owner of the off-licence where I got my first job. I worked hard and he was always smiling at me, so I thought he liked me and was happy with my work." Logan can feel her body tense but stays quiet allowing Catherine to tell him in her own way and in her own time. "I began to notice him watching me. I'd be putting stock away on the shelves and he'd pretend to be doing something, but I knew he was watching me." Her heart starts to pound as the image in her mind becomes clearer. "I began avoiding being alone with him – which was difficult as we didn't always have customers in the shop, but I stayed out front whenever possible."

A tear rolls unnoticed down her cheek and onto Logan's tightening chest. He has a very good idea of what is coming and his anger is rising. "It went on for a few weeks, but nothing ever happened; he didn't touch me or say anything to make me uncomfortable, but I was." Pulling the sheet more tightly around her, Logan feels Catherine burrow deeper into his side and tightens his arm around her. "It came from nowhere," her voice is distant now; "he was in a good mood, smiling, whistling or singing to a familiar tune. Then he said he was going out back for a fag and I actually smiled at him." She mumbles something that Logan struggles to hear, but it sounds like 'maybe that was it'. *I must have done something wrong.*

Pulling Catherine round to face him, Logan fights to keep the anger out of his voice, knowing it will only frighten her. "A smile is not an invitation to molest someone," he tells her firmly. "Whatever he did, he did because he wanted to and not because you did anything to encourage him." When she doesn't respond he gives her shoulders a gentle shake. "Catherine, you did nothing wrong."

Eyes wide and wet, Catherine stares back at Logan and shakes her head. *You don't know. No one knows.* "But I did," she sniffs, trying to hold back the tears but failing miserably, "I think I might even have killed him." *There, now you know you won't want me anymore!*

It is Logan's turn to go wide-eyed. "Just tell me what happened and don't leave anything out," he tells her. "Whatever it is, we can handle it."

Of course, she knows he is placating her, but Catherine also knows she can trust Logan; knows it from the bottom of her fearful heart. "He came in from his smoke break and seemed different, somehow. Like he'd made up his mind about something and was determined to do it - which, of course, he did. Or tried to," she amends grimly. "He didn't come straight at me; he moved towards the door and flipped the open sign to closed, then dropped the catch on the door."

Catherine closes her eyes tight on the memory then fights to carry on. "When he turned to face me his eyes were crazy looking and he was licking his lips like the dinner bell had rung. At first I froze, just stood there like a statue as he came towards me. Then I heard him, his voice sneering at me, 'that's right, little girl, I knew you wanted it, too', and before I could stop him he pushed me out into the stock room and up against the back wall." Her breathing is quickening now, and the tears roll freely down her cheeks. "He pushed his hands under my jumper, forcing my bra up and squeezed my breasts so hard I cried out in pain. That seemed to bring me back to my senses and I started to fight back, but he was so strong and I couldn't get free." *I couldn't get free. I couldn't get free.*

Her eyes plead for understanding, needing him to know that she hadn't wanted any of it to happen. "Then one hand was jammed down my trousers – the button flew off and the zip broke then his fingers were pushing inside me," she sobs brokenly, and presses a hand to her mouth holding back a scream. She is remembering the nightmare, the fear that what had happened to her mother was going to happen to her. *Mummy, please, I'm so scared. I'm so scared, mummy.*

That fear, clearly etched on her face, hurts Logan so deeply he can bear to see it no more. "Enough now!" He pulls her into his arms and rocks her while she weeps. "Shush, darling, don't cry – he can't hurt you anymore, I won't let him!" It is a vow Logan intends to keep; if Catherine hasn't killed him already he is going to pay Mr Shipley a visit he won't soon forget.

Eventually Catherine falls into an exhausted sleep. Gathering her up, Logan looks down at the woman in his arms and is amazed that all that courage is bottled up in so slight a body. Before laying her more comfortably on the bed, he raises his arms to place a kiss on her brow. Leaving the sheet where it is, still clutched tight against her, Logan pulls the quilt over Catherine and watches while she sleeps. Only when he is sure she isn't likely to wake does he get dressed and go down to see his father.

# Chapter Four

Henry is in the kitchen when Catherine goes down stairs. He has a bowl of eggs and milk he is whisking briskly.

"Wow, you really do cook," Catherine smiles. *Hope he's not mad that I missed supper.* "I felt sure you'd have a lovely Mrs Mop who cooked and cleaned for you."

Henry's grin is a mischievous version of Logan's, and she warms to him immediately. "Oh I can cook when I want to," he tells her, wagging the whisk like a pointy finger. "I used to help Ellie in the kitchen. Learned a lot from that woman; she was a dab hand at baking – won countless prizes at the local summer fare."

He isn't sad when he speaks of his late wife, Ellie, but he does have a longing in his voice, Catherine realises.

*You love her still.*

"So you manage this huge house all by yourself?" she asks, somewhat surprised.

Henry laughs a deep growling rumble that makes Catherine laugh too. "Wish I could say I do," he grins again, "but in all honesty Lakelands is far too big for me now. And my Mrs Mop is Aida Thorpe from the village. She's a gem, that woman, and no mistake. I wouldn't be able to stay on here without her help. But that's our little secret," he taps a finger to the side of his nose, "wouldn't do to let her head swell – she's bossy enough as it is." His laugh is infectious, and when Logan walks in, he finds them both still laughing.

"Sounds like that was a good joke," Logan takes in his father and Catherine's cheery faces, "care to share it?"

Putting a pan back on the range, Henry turns a warm smile on his son. "Come and share some breakfast with us instead, lad." Heaping scrambled eggs onto three plates Henry tops them off with piles of lean bacon and sliced grilled tomatoes that have Catherine's mouth salivating.

"If I eat all this I'll end up the size of a horse." Her eyes are wide as she picks up her knife and fork then tucks in eagerly. That first mouthful of eggs and bacon almost has her drooling. "Henry...this is amazing." Turning to Logan, she points her now empty fork at him. "Can you cook like this? 'cause I surely can't." *Bloody hell, this is fantastic!*

Henry laughs at Logan's stunned face. "Don't go frightening the lad," he admonishes Catherine kindly. "Logan never did like the kitchen. He always had his head in a book when he was a nipper." *Oh.*

"Sounds a lot like me," Catherine states, then frowns over at Logan. "So, you were different too, was it hard?" she asks, and he knows immediately what she means.

"No, Catherine, but then I'm not in your league," he states without a hint of judgement or resentment. *No, you didn't!* "It wouldn't have mattered which school you attended, you would always have stood out."

Henry watches the exchange with interest, noting Logan's careful tone and Catherine's stiffening.

"You've been checking up on me!" *Yes, you damned well did!* Her cutlery slams down and her chair is pushed back noisily.

He doesn't move to stand, but Logan looks up at Catherine curiously. "Are you seriously telling me that you didn't check up on me? Just a little background check?" He smiles when he sees the colour rise in her cheeks. "Thought so. With your computer skills I wouldn't be surprised to learn you had chapter and verse on me." Waving his fork, he indicates her chair. "Sit down and finish your breakfast, Catherine," he encourages. "You won't get another like it once we get back to Sheriton."

Pushing her food around her plate, Catherine watches Logan from beneath thick lashes.

*So, what did you find, Mr Nosey Git! And when are you going to tell me goodbye. No, perhaps not here – you'll wait until we get back, then dump me.*

Henry can see the situation isn't going to get any better with him sitting there, so he finishes off his breakfast quickly then takes his dishes over to the sink. Making his excuses, Henry goes out the back door and down the path to his chickens.

Moving over to the filter jug near the stove, Logan holds it up while looking back at Catherine. "Want some?"

She isn't exactly sulking, but Catherine is brooding about the search Logan has done on her. She nods for the coffee then gathers up the rest of the breakfast pots, scraping them off at the bin then putting them with Henry's in the sink.

"Let's take this outside," Logan suggests, handing Catherine a mug of wonderfully aromatic coffee. *So, this is it.*

They make their way round to the front terrace, which looks out towards the lake. The water is sparkling bright blue, reflecting the clear blue sky above it. There are no visual obstructions between the house and the lake, and Catherine has a feeling the expansive garden was planted to frame rather than obscure the view. *But what do I know.*

They sit quietly for a while, in the shade of the canopied veranda. "You didn't kill him, by-the-way." He can see that Catherine understands him; her head has spun round and her cheeks drained of all colour. *Oh my god!* "I made a few calls last night. You did put him in the hospital; but that was no more than he deserved," he stated derisively.

"But why no police?" she gasped in shocked amazement. *I've been waiting for the police to lock me up, for christ's sake!* For eight years, she had steered well clear of Granby Street afraid that someone would recognise her and turn her over to the police for murdering Shipley. *I didn't do it. I'm not a murderer. Oh god!*

Logan's brown eyes darken perceptibly, a dangerous glint in their depths. "The scumbag could hardly report the attack; if the police had spoken to you they would have heard your side of things, not something Shipley would have dared to let happen." His brow furrows and his eyes narrow, looking past Catherine and across the lake. "Especially as it wasn't his first time." He actually growls then, like a predator envisaging it's pray. *Not his first. Then maybe I really didn't make it happen.*

*Maybe.*

"I've hated myself for eight years thinking I'd killed that sack of shit," Catherine's fists clench in her lap, "now you tell me I didn't and I ought to be pleased; but somehow I'm really not!"

His own anger subsides when Logan looks over at Catherine. He can see the hate and disgust plainly in her eyes, but he can also see relief. "You wouldn't harm a fly if you didn't have to – it just isn't in you, Catherine."

She shakes her head. "It was in me eight years ago; what makes you so sure it isn't now?" *Even I don't know that. Won't ever really know that.*

He reaches over to loosen one of her fists so that he can hold her hand. "Because I've seen a side of you that no one ever has," his smile is tender, his chocolate brown eyes melting and soft. "No matter how hard you try to be the cold, hard Colson, you will always be the soft, warm Catherine inside."

"Don't be so sure," her chin lifts defiantly, "I've always said Catherine is a sissy name and you just confirmed it!" Her spine stiffens as she bristles. "I am not soft – when I want something I go after it and sod the people who get in my way. I will never be a victim, I will never allow it*!" Never! Never! Never!*

But you are, Logan thinks sadly. Whatever is eating away at you is making you a victim every day. To Catherine he says, "Always the little tough nut...," he smiles and gives her hand a shake, "...willing to take on the biggest, baddest bully in the playground." *Welcome to my world.*

"Of course...," Catherine frowns up at Logan, stymied, "...but that's not just me — that's life. If you show weakness in your business, how long will it take a competitor to start eating into it? It was the same in foster care; if you didn't stand your ground you lost it, and anything you thought you owned you suddenly didn't. And it wasn't just the bully who treated you like scum from then on," she recalls heatedly, "it was everyone in that place who had witnessed your weakness and prayed on it." *Never again! No one! Ever!*

"I'm sorry." Logan is only just beginning to understand how hard life has been for Catherine. His childhood had been idyllic. Most of it spent at Lakelands, until he'd boarded at Eton College and then at Oxford University. However, he has never been a stupid man. He has seen the bullies at work, and knows to what Catherine is referring. "I wish I could go back in time and change all those horrid memories for the good ones all children deserve..."

"But you can't," Catherine interrupts. "And don't feel sorry for me, I don't need it or want it. I am who I am and that's it – I'm just surprised you even like me, which I suppose you must if you put up with all the trouble that seems to comes with me." A grudging smile is tugging at her lips

*I can't believe you haven't dumped me. Maybe he doesn't know everything after all.*

He laughs, bringing their joined hands up to his lips. "Well, my life certainly hasn't been boring since you dropped into it." He smiles then, loving the pink that has crept into her cheeks. "As I'm sure you already know, I'm thirty-six years old; if I'd wanted boring I could have married one of the many suitable women in my social circle years ago." *I knew it was too good!* She looks up abruptly, her eyes so brightly blue. "You goose," he chucks her under her chin, making her smile, "I have no idea what you've done to me but I'm enjoying every minute of it." *Me too. I'm scared of just how much. It can't last.*

Her smile turns wistful, and her heart begins to open to the faint possibility of a little happiness in her tired life. "Could we go for a walk," she asks shyly, "I'd love to see your lake and the island?"

He stands, pulling Catherine to her feet with him. "We've always called it Ellie's island," he tells her, draping a companionable arm across her shoulders as hers circles his waist. "My mother fell in love with this place primarily because of the lake and the island at its centre. The house was just a place to live, as far as she was concerned."

"It sounds so romantic, your dad buying Lakelands just for your mum. He must have loved her very much." She smiles up at Logan, curious about his mother but not wanting to ask about what might still be a painful subject.

"We both did," he states, without sadness or grief. "We were lucky to have someone as kind and loving as my mother in our lives. She was a very special lady." He is looking out to the island now, across a lake that lies smooth as glass. "You see that old shack," he points at a small wood building that blends into the trees so well that Catherine wouldn't otherwise have noticed it. She nods, a hand shading her eyes from the bright sun the better to see it. "That's where my mother painted some of the pictures you'll see around the house," he tells her proudly.

"You're all so talented," Catherine muses. "My mum worked on the tills at a supermarket during the day, then did a couple of hours cleaning at night. That was for me," she adds as they sit on the grass near the lake's edge.

*I miss you so much, mum. You would have loved it here.*

"Did that bother you?" he asks quietly.

Catherine knows what he means, but no, she has never been ashamed of the work her mum has done. "Never!" she says adamantly. "My mum raised me on her own, worked six days a week plus two hours a night for five nights at the local school." Catherine turns fiercely proud eyes to Logan. "She did most of that for me so that I didn't go without. And we never owed a single penny to anyone; she was always firm on that. If we couldn't afford to pay for it we didn't have it – that was her philosophy all along, and one I'm proud to live by even now." *I'm sorry I was such hard work. I love you mum.*

"I'd have to say it's a good one," Logan nods. "It doesn't sound like your father is around much; why is that?" *Because he didn't want us!*

Catherine hesitates, decides that if the possibility of her being a bastard in the literal sense makes him balk, then so be it. Holding her head high she says, "Apart from the donation of his genes I didn't have a father." The statement is a challenge and Logan knows it, but he just smiles and waits for her to continue. Eyeing him warily, Catherine does continue. "I have no idea who he is, where he is, or even if he's still alive. And I don't care to," she adds defiantly. *He didn't care then and I don't care now!*

Brows creased, Logan asks the obvious question. "You're not even a little bit curious?"

Catherine's spine straightens. "Was he curious about me?" she states rather than asks. "He took off when he found out my mum was pregnant – no doubt crawled back under the same rock he crawled out of." *And bloody good riddance!*

"You sound so bitter, Catherine," he reaches for her hand but she pulls it quickly away to wrap her arms round her drawn up knees. "Do you really know for sure that your father didn't want or care for you? Things happen between couples that don't always end well," he urges, uneasy at her unbending attitude towards a man who just might deserve better.

Logan isn't blind to the fact that some parents do indeed walk at the first sign of trouble or responsibility; but he cannot understand why Catherine won't even entertain the prospect of finding out for herself who her father is and what kind of man he might be.

"I know he wasn't there for my mum when she needed him most!" Catherine gets to her feet and starts off, without looking back. Her long legs take her quickly along the water's edge, the calf length, lemon cotton dress fluttering in her wake. Then she breaks into a run and sprints out of site.

Logan doesn't attempt to stop or follow her. There is something eating away at Catherine, but he can't imagine what. Sure, she's had a bad start to life on her own, thanks to that bastard, Shipley, he growls audibly. But he didn't manage to actually rape her, though he isn't belittling the terror he had inflicted; hadn't he evidenced that himself just last night! He pushes up from the grass, needing to stretch his legs a while.

He thinks of Colson, the woman he was introduced to at Arthur and Robert's office just a couple of weeks ago. She'd had a strong, don't mess with me, attitude that wouldn't have allowed a shit like Shipley to get the better of her. Hell, hasn't she managed to live with the fear that she had actually killed the man for eight years – that is no mean feat. It just does not make sense, he reasons, jamming his hands in to the pockets of his slacks.

What had she meant about her mother? He knows she died when Catherine was still young; young enough to need foster care – but he hasn't delved deeply into her past, not wanting to invade Catherine's privacy beyond the basics.

He chuckles to himself. I'll just bet she didn't do a basic search on me, he thinks sceptically; and makes his way along the lake's edge in the opposite direction to Catherine.

It took her an hour or so to get rid of the knot in her stomach. Always physically painful, it could make her vomit when particularly bad. Doctor's had previously diagnosed a nervous stomach when her carers had forced her to go to one as a child. But she hadn't needed a doctor to tell her what it was; it always came when she thought of her mother, of the pain and suffering 'that man' had inflicted on her.

Taking a few deep, cleansing breaths, Catherine re-enters the house as she had left it, via the kitchen. There she finds a plump, pleasant looking woman, busy rolling pastry with pans of something delicious cooking on the stove. What a blissful scene.

"Hi, I'm Catherine," she introduces herself, not bothering to say Colson as both Logan and Henry insist on using her Christian name.

The cook looks up and smiles widely. "Yes, I heard from Henry that you'd be staying a few days; I made up your room," she says in a conspiratorial whisper, "can't leave such things to Henry, he hasn't got a clue. Don't know what he'd do if I didn't come in to look after things." *Really?*

Catherine smiles, remembering Henry's earlier comments about the 'bossy' Aida Thorpe. She watches as Aida wipes her hands on a damp cloth then takes the kettle to the sink to fill it. "I'm Aida, by the way. Don't suppose Henry thought to mention me?" *Oh yes he did.* Catherine manages to stifle a laugh but can't hide the smile or the knowing twinkle in her eyes before Aida turns back from the sink and catches them. "So...he did mention me," she eyes Catherine speculatively. "Not all of it complimentary I see."

She sounds brusque, but Catherine can see she doesn't mean it. "Actually, it was," she lies convincingly, "he obviously relies on you quite a bit." She consoles herself that she hasn't actually said that Henry has said as much to her in confidence, so she isn't really betraying him. She hopes.

Aida's head lifts in pride. "I knew it," she states with a smug smile and setting the kettle on the range to boil. "He always makes out like he's the one doing me a favour, what with me being a widower and needing the job; but I can tell when a place needs a woman's touch. Not that Henry's lazy or fuddled like some older folk get," she smiles fondly, obviously not putting herself in that category either, "he's just a typical man. He can't think like a woman because he isn't one," and that seems to be explanation enough to Aida's way of thinking. *And you care about him very much.*

Catherine chuckles then. "Is Henry still out in the back garden?" she asks, knowing that is where he disappeared to after breakfast.

"No, no...," Aida's head is bent over the pastry she has begun to roll out again, "...he's away in the library – just down the hall, second door on the left – I'll bring you both a cup of tea when the kettle's boiled."

Catherine finds Henry studying a large book spread out over a desk. Giving a knock on the already open door, Catherine smiles as he looks up. "Aida told me where to find you," she tells him as she crosses the room. "She also said she'd bring us a cup of tea in; that's if I'm not disturbing you?" Her smile is uncertain now.

"Not at all," Henry waves her over. "I'm just looking at the old plans for this place."

Catherine looks with interest at the old intricate blueprints for the Lakelands house and grounds. "Henry, these are amazing." She moves to his side to get a better look. *Probably worth a small fortune but obviously worth more than mere money to Henry.* "Are you thinking of making some kind of alterations to the house?" she asks, as these are the pages he appears to be studying.

He looks a bit flustered. "Well...I don't know...needs change...and, one day...maybe..." Catherine actually sees a spot of red come in to Henry's cheeks. "...well, Logan may want to make this his home, too," he declares quickly.

*Oh you thoughtful, lovely man.*

She smiles wickedly. "You haven't told Logan about this, have you?"

"No I haven't," he replies, closing the book and putting it back on the shelf, "and I'd appreciate it if you didn't mention it to him."

Aida wheels a tea trolley in then, and tells them that lunch will be ready in about an hour. After pouring two cups of tea and setting the small plate of biscuits, that Aida has thoughtfully provided, on the table between them, Catherine takes a seat opposite Henry and considers his request.

"I can't imagine why you wouldn't want Logan to know about your plans for the house?" she asks, frowning over her teacup. "I mean, how great is that, to have a dad who would go to all that expense and trouble to entice you back home?"

*I wish I had a dad like you – mine probably doesn't even know I'm alive.*

"Mmm," Henry smiles crookedly, "you'd think so, hey?"

Catherine's smile falters a bit, realising that she still hasn't done what she originally came for. "Actually, Henry, I came here to apologise for this morning. I shouldn't have made you so uncomfortable in your own home that you felt you had to leave it." *I'm such an idiot.*

"I only went to feed the chickens," he offers, then sees that she isn't buying that. "Well, couples sometimes need a little privacy to work things out. I know Ellie and I had our moments; life would get a tad boring without a few fireworks to liven things up now and then." His smile is wide and sincere, and Catherine loves him for it.

"Is that how you see us?" She asks tentatively. "As a couple, I mean."

Henry looks surprised. "Don't you?"

*It's too soon. It won't last. But I want it to. He's the best thing to ever happen to me.*

Catherine frowns for a moment. "But we've known each other for such a short time; isn't it a little early to be thinking like that?"

"Humph," Henry gruffs loudly. "Knew how I felt about Ellie the first time I saw her; but you youngsters – always analysing and pulling everything to pieces before you even half way trust it. Go with your gut," he states uncompromisingly, "that's what I say."

"It's a fine idea," she hesitates, "I'm just not sure that my gut is as trustworthy as yours appears to be." *Or as deserving.*

Henry studies Catherine for a long minute. "You're the first he's ever brought home; that's all I'll say." Then Henry stands up and waves Catherine over to the back wall of the library. "A little inside information," he winks as he indicates the many photos displayed there.

Still digesting that titbit of information that has caused her stomach to do a back flip, Catherine follows him. "Are all these of Logan?" she asks, amazed to see him holding up trophies of one type or another in each of the photos.

"Not all. I've got some of Ellie up there," Henry, points to the right hand corner of the display, "she won more than one trophy or rosette for her baking; and proud of them she was, too."

Going from one to the other, Catherine is fascinated by the photos of Logan between the ages of about five to in his teens, or early twenties. It is difficult to tell, as he has evidently always been tall.

"He was good at just about any sport; athletics, rugby, football and swimming were his favourites, though," Henry continues, then points to a photo of Logan in swimming trunks; all arms and legs and gangly looking. "That's when he won the swimming gold cup – ordinarily it is silver, but they gave him a gold one for winning it three years in a row." Catherine glances up to see a proud gleam in Henry's eyes. Then he points over to a glass cabinet. "We saved all his trophies, and Ellie's, too." Turning back to the wall of photos, he reaches up to draw a gentle finger over the face of an elegant looking woman. "My Ellie," he whispers, and Catherine is sure he has, momentarily, forgotten her presence. "We were so proud of our boy, weren't we?"

*To be loved like that. How many people are that lucky?*

Catherine shifts, intending to leave Henry with his memories of Ellie, but he turns and she sees that his eyes are glistening. "Logan and I were devastated when Ellie passed away. I can only thank the Lord that he took her quickly. Cancer can be a terrible death, but we found out why she had been so tired and listless one month and she died the next. Her ashes are sprinkled on the island at the centre of the lake, just as she asked." He turns then to see Logan enter the room, knowing he has heard his sad lament. "And of course, I'd be content to join my Ellie on her island if this one would stop making it his life's work to stay a bachelor."

Logan laughs, comfortable with his father's teasing. It isn't the first time after all. "Aida sent me to tell you both that lunch is ready and she's served it up on the front terrace as it's such a lovely day." He walks over to Catherine as his father strides out of the library. Holding his arm out to her, like the gentlemen of old, he asks, "May I escort a lady to lunch?" *You idiot.*

"You could if there were any ladies in the room," she giggles, but puts her arm through his anyway, grateful that they are no longer at odds.

"I think I should take umbrage at that," he says with mock severity, "as I seem to remember picking that particularly lovely dress out myself."

Not used to compliments or dresses, Catherine blushes deeply. "You picked them all out," she reminds him, hiding her face against his arm. "I'm well aware that I don't have any taste or style, or whatever the bloody hell every other woman has; but I have to admit, I like this one." Logan beams. She gives a yank on his arm. "No need to look so smug, it's just a dress." *But I'm so glad you like it.*

"Don't get all defensive," Logan chides, bringing them both to a stop in the hallway. "You look beautiful, and I adore you." *Oh!*

Catherine can hardly catch her breath; after this morning, she thought she had ruined everything. "You do?"

"I absolutely do," he confirms, before pulling her into his arms to kiss her.

She's so thrilled, and relieved, that Catherine pours her heart and soul into the kiss and Logan responds in kind. Holding him, having him hold her, it makes her so happy. So very happy. *And he tastes so damn good!*

A discreet cough at the end of the hallway has them springing apart. It is Aida, and she is trying not to smile. "Your lunch'll be getting cold. It's only a dressed salad but I put some hot chicken and new potatoes with it."

They look at each other, caught like a couple of teenagers snogging behind the bike sheds at school, and break into fits of laughter that has Catherine bent over double

## <u>Chapter Five</u>

Tall and lean, Catherine makes a lovely vision in her short pink and grey dress, Logan observes as he watches her standing on the terrace looking out at Ellie's island. Her drastically short blonde hair, though it is starting to grow enough on top to flutter slightly in the breeze, doesn't detract from her beauty in his eyes. He imagines she stands around five feet nine or ten, still below shoulder height to him in her bare feet, but then most women are he concedes. He walks towards her, making sure she will hear him coming so as not to startle her out of her reverie. "Penny for them?"

Catherine's cheeks pink prettily as she remembers her daydreams of Logan. "Not worth it," she dismisses. "I was only thinking about work," she lies unconvincingly.

*What a body!*

"Well...," Logan chuckles, "...if thinking of work puts that colour in your cheeks I'd love to see what thinking of us does to you." He moves in for a kiss and she puts her arms around his neck instinctively. "Mmm," he groans, as their lips part, still holding her in the circle of his arms, "you taste as good as you look." His eyes are warm and staring right in to hers. *What do you see in me? Can you see the ugliness inside...?*

She smiles up at him, her blue eyes bright with tentative hope and a love she still has not admitted to, even to herself. "That's all you get for now, big boy," she murmurs, and makes to move out of his arms, but Logan is not letting her go.

"For now...?"He repeats suggestively. "Does that mean you have plans for us for later?" His hands move down from her waist to her bottom, and pull her to him intimately.

"Logan!" Catherine is more than a little pink, now she is mortified. "Henry...," she splutters looking warily back at the house. *Bloody hell!*

His quiet laughter does nothing to lessen her embarrassment, but he does drop his hold on her then takes her hand instead. "Let's go for a walk," he invites, not even attempting to hide his intentions from her.

Her heart leaps into her throat, her breathing suddenly laboured, but she moves with him willingly. *And they say dreams are just wishes the heart makes – I'll have to daydream more often!*

Halfway towards the lake and its surrounding trees and gardens, Henry calls out to Logan. "You've got a visitor, son." *Fuck!*

Logan takes Catherine's face between gentle hands. "I think I know who it is and this shouldn't take long." He takes the time to kiss her until her pulses race, and then breaks away reluctantly. "Remember my place, we're just getting started," he smiles evocatively.

She watches his long muscular legs eat up the ground to the house and thinks his arse looked good enough to sink her teeth in to. Catherine laughs to herself, suddenly feeling all hot and bothered and knowing it has nothing to do with the glorious sunshine. *Hurry back, Logan. Phew!*

However, Logan's business with the visitor has taken a long time. Long enough that Catherine has made her way back to the terrace and is sipping a glass of iced orange juice, freshly prepared for her by the inestimable Aida. With the French windows open, she can clearly hear Logan outlining a property refurbishment deal to someone. It doesn't sound to Catherine like he is talking about doing up just any little building, not with the huge amounts of money she's heard him mention. *Mmm, I wonder if Logan can find us some new office premises at a reasonable price. If any prices can be called reasonable these days!*

Then she hears the visitor speak for the first time, his Welsh accented voice deep and distinctive. She stands reflexively, the glass slipping unnoticed from her hand. Walking backwards, she stumbles off the terrace on to the surrounding grass and freezes, completely immobile.

That voice! *This one's a beauty; I can cut toes off in a blink, watch. No, no, Oh God, please no. See, now listen to those lovely screams – that's what real pain sounds like, little girl. I can't breathe...I can't...*

She hasn't even noticed their conversation conclude; hasn't stopped hearing the sound of that voice...that voice...that voice, her mind repeats as her world rocks beneath her bare feet.

"What the hell!" Logan rushes forward, takes hold of Catherine's stone cold shoulders and gives them a gentle shake. "Catherine, what is it?"

As she follows Logan's glance down her body, Catherine realises that her bare legs and feet are now soaked in her own urine. "Oh my god!" She cries out on the verge of hysteria. Then a hand flies up to cover her mouth, her eyes going wide as that voice, that terrible voice, reverberates around in her confused thoughts. *I'm sorry, mummy. I'm so sorry...*

Before Logan can stop her, Catherine dashes off into the house, up the stairs to her bedroom and locks the door safely behind her. She barely makes it to the bathroom in time, vomiting as if her insides will tear at the force of it. When it finally subsides, Catherine can only think of a shower. She can hear Logan hammering on the bedroom door demanding to be let in. Were it a less sturdy door it surely would have given way. But she can't focus on Logan right now, can't even comprehend how frantic he must be after finding her in such a state. Lifting her face into the warm spray of the shower, Catherine slowly lowers herself to the floor of the cubicle. She sobs a million tears, each one clearing away the mist that has hung over the buried memories of her mother.

She was hiding in her mother's bedroom under the bed. The noise of someone breaking into the house downstairs had terrified her. She had hoped and prayed that he would take whatever he wanted quickly then go before her mum came home; but Catherine's prayers hadn't been answered. She'd heard her mum calling for her, becoming increasingly impatient when she got no reply. Then there was a scuffle, her mother screamed but the sound was cut off suddenly and Catherine held her breath in fear. Then she heard heavy feet on the stairs and the bedroom door had opened; Catherine had clapped both hands over her mouth to stop any noise escaping then had to listen as the man dumped her mum's body on the bed and began tying her to it.

"I tried, mummy..." Catherine, hands clasped around her knees, rocks herself with the pain of remembering, "...I tried to warn you that he was there; but it wouldn't come out. My voice just wouldn't come out," she sobs for her mother over and over. Then, finally, when the only water tumbling down her face is the spray from the shower, Catherine draws herself up, wraps a large towel about her and moves robotically to the wardrobe.

Downstairs Henry is trying to calm Logan, telling him to give her some space and time. "She's stronger than you give her credit for," Henry states confidently. "Catherine has taken care of herself just fine up till now and you ought to just let her calm down, then we'll see what's what."

"I need to leave now," Catherine states simply, quietly, standing at the foot of the stairs and taking them both by surprise. Both men turn in their seats to look at her, their heads whipping round in unison as if she has just yelled at them. "I can call a taxi," she offers when neither of them moves, "I really don't mind."

For the last couple of hours, Logan has been wearing a groove in his father's hallway after trying to break the bedroom door down hadn't worked. He was desperate to talk to her, wanting her to explain what the hell happened in the short time he'd left her alone. However, looking at Catherine, he can see that any explanations will have to wait. Her face is ghost-like, shut down, blank of all emotion.

"Come and sit down for a minute, Catherine," he invites, rising to his feet as she continues to stand at the foot of the stairs. "I'll have to bring the car round first." But Catherine doesn't move, or blink. Logan makes his way slowly towards her, but knows instinctively that now is not the time to offer comfort or any physical contact. Instead, he gets the car, stows the few bags that Catherine has brought down with her in the boot, then says goodbye to his father, promising to ring him later that night.

The drive back to Sheriton is not as enjoyable as the trip down had been. The tension in the air is heavy enough to cut with a knife, but Catherine just doesn't know where to begin.

As if she has said the words aloud, Logan asks her to tell him only what she can. "You don't need to go into specifics," he encourages, trying to make it as easy for her as possible.

The fact that he is driving and has to concentrate on the narrow country lanes means he won't so easily be able to turn to look at her; to see the horror of the nightmare on her face, and she takes some comfort in that.

"I'm not sure that I can anyway," she tells him, "I've tended to push it all to the back of my mind." Catherine expects Logan to chime in with some words of encouragement or empty platitudes. She's heard them all as she was growing up. "I was at home on my own," she begins. "My mum was out doing the cleaning job I told you about. I was nine, almost ten, so it was no big deal. I'd watch the telly, or more likely read one of my many books." She surprises herself by smiling and Logan hears it in her voice. "One of the reasons my mum took the extra work was to keep me supplied with endless books. I was hard work, you see."

Catherine falls silent recalling her mum's futile attempts to occupy her. But she had grown bored quickly, had become sullen and cheeky or gone off on long walks round the neighbourhood. Anyway, she knows it hadn't been easy for her mum; until she'd discovered books, that is. And not the usual junior novels like all the other kids read. No, hers had been expensive textbooks. *As if life wasn't difficult enough for mum.*

"Catherine...?" is all Logan needs to say.

"I couldn't get enough books," she begins again. "Not stories or novels," she dismisses with a snort of disgust, "but real books; about how things work and why. I mean, at nine you not only want to know who invented the modern jumbo jet, or how it's put together, but how it manages to stay up there in the clouds with all those people and luggage and other things that should make it too heavy even to leave the ground, let alone fly thousands of feet above it." She is smiling again, he knows, and is glad for her to have those precious memories as well as the horrors that she still hasn't spoken of. Is she stalling, he wonders.

"My mum marvelled at the things I came out with – see what this does, mum – or, look what that does, mum – and, look how this works, mum" *So selfish. So completely self-absorbed.* Catherine shakes her head in wonder at her mother's patience. "So...you can see how buying books that gave me all the information I seemed to crave became the easier option; and working evenings gave her a break from me anyway." *She needed it.*

"Yet Arthur Kingsley told me that you had never been to university," Logan interjects. "Was he wrong...?"

"No he wasn't wrong." Then she tells him about being called a freak at school. And about the bloody noses the other kids' parents had regularly complained that their children were coming home with. "I was happiest on my own," he hears her continue. "I didn't need any of them. But my mum couldn't understand it when the school complained about my behaviour and my inability to interact during lessons. I'd become the model child at home, you see. As for exams," she flicks them off with a sharp wave of her hand, "I just refused to do them." *Refused to tow their bloody line. Fuckers!*

"But, why?" he asks, suddenly confused. "You could have done anything, gone to university and been anything you wanted to be."

"Yeah," she scoffs, "if I'd just played the game the way they wanted it played. 'We're reading The Lord of the Rings just now, dear,'" she mimics, doing her best impression of the redoubtable Miss Parish, her English teacher. "Then she confiscated the book I was reading and forced me to read the book she wanted me to read out loud in front of the whole class." She actually crosses her arms over her chest in a move that brings a smile to Logan's face. One that, the now angry, Catherine has noticed. "Oh I suppose you were Mr Popular," she scoffs acidly. "Always the little gentleman; yes sir, no sir, three bags bloody full sir.” *Jesus-H-Christ! A right Little Lord fucking Fauntleroy!*

Logan actually laughs out loud at that, and Catherine's scowl deepens. “I was no saint, I assure you,” he tells her, still chuckling at her description of him. “But learning never did come easy to me, so I had to discipline myself to study hard and pay attention in class. Not all of us have blotting paper for brains,” he counters.

“Were you always set on going to university then?” she asks. “Or did you get pushed along the way by your parents?”

“You've met my father – does he seem like the pushy parent type to you?”

Catherine thinks that over. No, Henry had not seemed like that at all. But then what did she know about fathers, she'd never had one. “I don't have any experience in the father department,” she states matter of fact. “But I wouldn't have said that Henry is pushy, not in an overbearing way anyway,” she clarifies.

“But you think he could be in other ways...?” He is genuinely interested in her opinions, and is enjoying their frank exchange; though he knows he is facilitating her stalling tactics at the same time.

“I think he'd have kicked your arse black and blue if you'd cheeked him the way I used to cheek my mum.” She turns to smile at him, but it falters and dies, leaving her looking sad. *My mum ought to have given me the back of her hand. I never deserved her. So loving. So patient. So...*

"Is that what your mum did?" he probes gently. "Did your mother hurt you, Catherine? Is that what you're remembering?"

She tells him everything then. "My mum was the kindest person you could ever wish to meet, and she rarely laid a hand on me; though I deserved it sometimes." Her lips tremble on the pitiful smile they try to form. "I was the child from hell," she tells him frankly. "No matter what she tried to do with me – be it puzzles, or reading stories, or taking me out to the park – it was never enough to satisfy me. Although physical activities, like swimming and track running, did help as long as I drove myself hard enough to reach near exhaustion." *Even that had been a short-term solution.*

He glances over at her. "I think I remember reading something about that, though not strictly in the same context," Logan tells her. "It had to do with children who had Attention Deficit Disorder and how to channel all that extra energy they seem to have into positive, rather than destructive activities."

Catherine nods in agreement. "I suppose there are valid comparisons to be made. After all, I did have an attention deficit, the fact that it was caused by mind numbing boredom didn't change the outcome of it. I was still loud and angry, or subdued and shutdown, for most of the time. I could go from one extreme to the other in minutes; my poor mum didn't know which way to turn." Her voice has grown quieter, her memories harder to bear. "I loved her so much," her lips tremble but she will not give in to the tears. Stiffening her resolve, she asks Logan, "How much do you already know about me – you did a background check, so you must at least have the basics?"

"The 'basics' is about right," he tells her. "I didn't go further than your senior educational background really. That gave me your age and the fact that you transferred schools a few times. Any more than that is just hearsay; like Arthur and Robert, they both speak very highly of you." He frowns over at Catherine, "I really did just do a surface run and only because I was curious, and wanted to get to know you." *Wanted. Yes, I'll soon be in the past tense once I get through telling you what a nut job you've hooked up with!*

"That's it?" She asks. "You didn't look into my family background or my earlier education?" *I don't know why I'm even bothering to ask. If you had you'd have run a mile. Maybe you still will. Oh, Jesus!*

"No," he reiterates softly. "What would I have found if I had?" Out of the corner of his eye, he can see Catherine brace herself and knows that whatever she is about to say is going to hurt her deeply.

"You were thirty six a couple of months ago," she states matter-of-fact. "That would have made you twenty when I was still nine going on ten." Catherine doesn't notice his heavy sigh at hearing that bit of revelatory math, she is too busy putting her remembered facts into some relevant order. "Do you remember hearing about the murder of a woman named Sara Colson? It was a deliberate home invasion; he came prepared so it was obviously premeditated."

Logan pales visibly. "Good lord! I didn't put it together – she was your mother?" he gasps.

Catherine nods; it will help that he already knows the gist of what happened. "The newspapers were pretty graphic in their reporting," she states unemotionally, "so you must know that she was raped and tortured to death." *And I did nothing to stop him! Fucking coward!*

Logan cannot believe his own stupidity, it had been all anyone had talked about for months afterwards. His own father had become very protective of his mother, ferrying her to this place and that and always insisting on picking her up afterwards. "Yes," he admits, a note of deep disgust in his voice, "it was sickening just to hear about; I couldn't bring myself to actually read it." Though, the ghouls who'd enjoyed reading every detail also enjoyed talking about it. This meant he hadn't been able to escape the vile gossip.

"Well...one thing you wouldn't have read about is the fact that I was there, the whole time." *Sick bastard!* Her face and tone become stony, totally detaching herself from her emotions.

Logan's hands tighten on the steering wheel; his head reeling with shock. He pulls the car over at the first opportunity and sits in stunned silence.

When he eventually speaks, it is to ask a question more out of hope than to hear the answer. "You mean you were hiding somewhere in the house and he didn't know?" *Yes, that would make a much nicer, more sanitised tale.*

She doesn't turn to look at him, already knowing what she'll see if she does. "Yes...and no," she replies cryptically. "I did hide, under my mother's bed, but he found me. In fact, he dragged me out by my feet after he'd finished raping my mother on her bed."

"Oh god!" *Is that disgust? I'm not surprised.* His head falls forward to rest his forehead on the steering wheel.

"Did he hurt you – I know he didn't rape you – but did he hurt you?"

Catherine finds the strength to look over at Logan and is actually shocked to see the depth of his pain on her behalf. Reaching out a hand, she prises his off the steering wheel and holds it in both of hers. "If you mean did he do to me what he did to my mother, no, he didn't."

Logan looks over at her, and knows there is more to come. "You don't have to tell me, Catherine. I don't want to put you through any more pain."

She gives his large hand a squeeze, managing to offer him some small comfort. "The pain will be there whether I tell you or not; maybe it'll even help to finally talk about it." *I've never been able to get the words out, and never wanted to tell the authorities, they hadn't really cared about my mum!*

"But surely, you must have told the police, and no doubt the social workers, everything that happened?" Logan frowns quizzically.

She shakes her head. "I didn't speak a word to anyone for two years," she explains. "And, as I'd attacked the social worker they brought in to look after me, they locked me up in a psychiatric unit – they thought the trauma of it all had sent me loopy," she scoffs scathingly, remembering the psychiatrists discussing her like she wasn't in the room, assuming she couldn't hear just because she couldn't speak. *Fuckheads!*

"I'm so sorry, Catherine, I had no idea." He is looking at her, and he can see that she is searching his face for any signs of pity. "You are, without doubt, one of the strongest, most resourceful women I have ever had the pleasure to meet. You astound me!"

*If only I could believe you will still feel that way after you hear all of this.*

"I need to finish this, Logan," she states quietly. "I have to get it over with while I have at least a modicum of control..." she squeezes the hand she is still holding, "...and you give me that." *For now, at least.*

He uses that hand to pull her towards him; putting his arms around her and wishing he could transfer all his strength to Catherine, knowing she is going to need it. "I don't know about you," he smiles, and drops a kiss on the top of her head, "but I really needed that."

Catherine smiles, and puts her hand on his cheek. "I don't know how or why, but you've become my rock and, yes, I needed that too." *Very much.*

They sit back in their seats, still holding hands. "Ok," she breathes. "So, now you know that my mum's name was Sara and that she was murdered in the worst way imaginable." After a couple of steadying breaths, she continues. "Now I'm going to tell you what the newspapers couldn't. After he'd finished raping my mother he reached under the bed and grabbed my ankles, then hauled me out and threw me over his shoulder like a sack of spuds." Her eyes go distant and Logan knows she is seeing it all again. "He probably didn't care, but from that position I could see my mum – he'd used duct tape to bind her hands and feet, one to each corner of the bed and a piece across her mouth to keep her quiet. But it didn't," she recalls. "Even while I was hiding under the bed, too witless to do anything to help her, I heard her screams while he raped her; and I would hear them a lot more throughout that night." *I still hear them.*

Catherine rubs her free hand over her eyes and squeezes them together as if trying to erase the memory. "I thought he was taking me to my bedroom; was terrified he was going to do to me what he'd already done to my mum," she meets Logan's eyes then, "but he didn't. He just picked up the chair at my desk and carried it and me back to my mum's bedroom. Then he made me sit on it and used the duct tape to fasten each of my ankles to the outside of the two front legs of the chair," she swallows hard, "I was totally exposed, though I still had my pants on, but he looked directly up my skirt and laughed. Then he pulled my arms to the back of the chair and bound my hands so that I couldn't move, and all this time I hadn't made a noise."

She blinks rapidly and stares at Logan. "I don't remember making a noise even when I was under the bed, but I suppose I must have for him to have known I was there." She gives herself a mental shake to bring back her focus. "We were both helpless, now, so he could move about the house as he pleased. My mum looked over at me, tears streaming from her eyes, and I knew she was trying to tell me that she was sorry." She laughs derisively then. "Can you believe it, I'm the one who did nothing to help her and she was apologising to me!"

*Forgive me, mum...because I can't. I never will!*

Logan puts his hand to her face and gently turns Catherine to face him. "Neither you nor your mother are to blame for anything that monster did!" he tells her quietly but firmly. "And you were nine years old, what the hell do you think you could have done that would have changed anything? He was a madman; if you had caused him even the smallest grief things could have taken an even nastier turn than they did – do you honestly think your mum would have wanted that?" he asks, deliberately referring to her mother as Catherine did.

"I tried," she tells him, and a single tear escaped her eyes to tumble unnoticed down her cheek, "when I heard her key in the door I heard myself screaming to her to get out, but my voice was only in my head – it wouldn't come out, no matter how I tried, it wouldn't come out."

"And you didn't speak again for two years?" he asks.

Catherine shakes her head. "I don't know if I could have, I never tried. There was no reason to anymore," she states softly, "and what would I have said if I had. My head was full of remembering – the table he brought into the bedroom, the way he laid out all his instruments of torture in perfectly neat rows, and the way he described to me exactly what he was going to do with each one before using it so brutally on my mum." Her face looks quizzically at Logan, then. "He actually enjoyed every moment of my mum's pain and was ecstatic when I peed my pants; said it was a sign that he'd achieved ultimate terror." Catherine closes her eyes and shakes her head, "If I live to be a hundred, I'll never understand the why of it."

Catherine is exhausted; Logan can see it all over her. She can barely hold herself upright in her seat. He reaches across her to check the tension on her seatbelt then says, "I'm taking you home, Catherine. You've been through enough, now." She makes to protest but Logan is adamant. "Look at you, you're dead beat; and don't deny it," he warns. "I'm taking you home and you'll get some rest. Then, if you think it's necessary, you can fill me in on the rest." However, he hopes earnestly for her sake that the worst is over.

"Oh, it'll be necessary," she tells him, a cold edge of steel lining her voice.

## Chapter Six

Well, he had asked for it and Catherine had told him, all of it. Even down to that distinctive voice, she had thought she recognised on the terrace of Lakelands.

No wonder Catherine was paralysed with fear to the point where she lost control of her bladder. The very thought that a man like that was anywhere near-by would have been enough to terrify anyone.

But surely, it couldn't have been Charles Llwyd she had witnessed torturing her mother to death as a child. He's known Charles for years; had sold him his current home in the neighbouring village of Upper Stanton. Logan sits in the drawing room of his large detached home, contemplating the almost unthinkable possibilities.

Charles is in his early sixties now, so, that would have made him in his late forties fifteen years ago when

Catherine was nine. Though she said that she'd been almost ten, he recalls, wanting to get the facts straight in his mind. But the man Catherine described had been much younger – so had she been wrong? Had she remembered the attacker's voice wrong, after so many years and having been so young and traumatised when she'd heard it in the first place? But then he has to consider Catherine's brilliant memory. Perhaps it isn't just facts and figures that her brain absorbs so readily. Perhaps she has perfect recall of other things, too.

Catherine has not been home or to her office for over a week. Not since Logan drove them, back from Lakelands and insisted that she at least stay the night. Settling Catherine in her own room, Logan insisted that she hang the clothes she brought back with her, up in the wardrobe.

Now she is restless; Logan has had to go into his office today and she is left on her own to continue their work on finding the animal that murdered her mother. Perhaps I ought to phone Ben again she ponders a frown drawing her brows together, and moans aloud at the prospect. She couldn't blame him; when he learned that she'd been back for three days before she had even thought to ring him, he'd been righteously pissed! He hadn't quite handed his notice in, but she is sure it had been a close run thing.

"Well here goes," she says to the empty room, and picks up the phone in the lounge to call him. "Ben, hi," she greets him cheerily, though it sounds forced even to her, "I thought we could catch up over lunch," she offers, "If you'd like to?"

He volunteers to pick her up, and although she doesn't want to admit that she is still at Logan's house, she doesn't have her car so has to accept. "Ok, that's fine." *Bloody hell!* Catherine gives him Logan's address and ignores the muttered oath that Ben doesn't even try to smother. "I'll see you at one, then, bye."

Going back to Logan's home office, Catherine sits back down behind his desk and studies the screen of his computer.

"Now then, where did we get to?" she asks, talking to herself. "Yes, that's it." She reads an article about a murder that had happened ten years ago – Logan thought it might be connected, reasoning that even if the modus operandi was different the level of violence is a match, and she has to agree. However, they have actually found sixty-three murders committed over the last fifteen years that match the criteria they have set. *Sick fucks!* They enter all of them onto a spreadsheet, detailing age and sex of victim, injuries sustained, duration of attack, marital status, how many children they had, and whether or not the killer has been apprehended.

Having finished the article, Catherine sits back in the chair and pushes her hands back through her hair. "Jesus...it's a fucked up world." When she thinks about all the families affected by the murder of a loved one, she considers herself lucky in a twisted kind of a way. After all, it has just been her, no husband or brothers and sister to worry about – just her.

Diving back into her search, Catherine doesn't notice the passage of time and starts violently when the doorbell rings. "Christ, is that the time?"

Preparing herself before opening the door, Catherine repeats the words 'I am calm' in her head then plasters a greeting smile on her face. "Hi, Ben, I'm all ready, just let me get my bag."

Ben doesn't reply at first. "What the hell are you wearing?"

She freezes, having forgotten that she is wearing one of the dresses she bought on her recent shopping trip with Logan. "It's a bloody dress, Ben," she spits out defensively. "Women wear them!"

"Not you," he states matter-of-fact. "So I'm guessing it's a present from Logan, as you're near as damn it living with the chap lately." He sounds petulant and knows it but doesn't care.

"As it happens I bought it and a few others myself," she tells him, feeling guilty because it isn't the whole truth. "Now, if you've finished your critique of my clothing I'll get my bag and we can go." *Dresses, I should have known!*

Ben goes to wait in the car. Catherine is furious with herself for not remembering she is wearing her favourite long yellow summer dress. Now she feels stupid in it and wishes she had her comfortable tops and tracky bottoms. Grabbing up her bag she leaves a note for Logan in case he gets back before she does. *Christ, it's as bad as being married*!

Climbing into Ben's car feels awkward. She doesn't know why, she's been in it many times and Ben is a good friend – but it just doesn't feel right. "So where are we going for lunch?" she asks, trying to sound perky.

"Did you really buy that dress?" is Ben's only reply.

*For fucks sake!*

Catherine sighs deeply. "Yes, Ben, I did, and if all you're going to talk about is this fucking dress then you can take me back right now!"

But his demeanour suddenly brightens. "Actually, I fancy going to the Horse and Hound," he states as if she hasn't spoken, "they've got a lovely garden area – we can eat alfresco."

She doesn't actually turn to stare at him, but Catherine does eye him warily. "That sounds great," she frowns, forcing a smile, "it'll be nice to have a chance to sit out in this lovely weather." *Weird!*

Pulling into the car park, Ben finds an empty space not too far from the front. "There we go," he smiles as they both alight the car. Then he turns to look at Catherine. "You know, that dress really does look nice on you. You should wear them more often."

Catherine's inner voice is telling her that he probably wouldn't think so if he knew that Logan had paid half for it; but decides to keep that her little secret. "Thank you. As it happens I picked up a few more at the same time, so perhaps I will."

Considering the topic of conversation, Catherine decides that the meal has gone well. "I'm glad you don't mind handling things for another couple of days; I knew I could rely on you," and she genuinely feels some of the old warmth of their friendship rekindling.

"Not a problem," Ben assures her, glad that she feels able to lean on him, "but I do wish you would trust me enough to tell me what the trouble is you're trying to sort out – perhaps I can help?" *Oh, lord, now what?*

They are walking back to the car and Catherine tries to refuse his offer of help without hurting his feelings. "It's nothing I can't handle, Ben, but if I need you I'll get in touch."

"Just make sure you do," he tells her.

Back at Logan's house, Catherine realises she can't get in. Mrs Baines has gone home for the day and Logan is still at work. Glad that Ben has driven straight off, she settles herself on the doorstep to wait, but after half an hour decides to go for a walk in the rear grounds.

At the back of the house, the garden is glorious. *Whoever designed this*, she thinks while sauntering along a concealed pathway, *is a bloody genius*.

She finds a small pergola with established plants forming walls and a roof over an arrangement of seating. She sits and thinks about Logan, and about what they have been doing over this last week. He still isn't convinced that Charles Llwyd, the man she overheard him talking to at Lakelands, is her mother's murderer. *Yes, he has known the man for years and he is, apparently, a happily married man - but so was Peter Sutcliffe, the latter day Jack-The-Ripper, happily married according to his wife*, she reasons. *It seems she hadn't had a clue what he was up to either. So how can Logan be so sure?*

Catherine goes over and over what they have discovered on the internet and their discussions about Llwyd; but it all comes back to that voice.

*'Just watch what this one does,'* he'd taunted Catherine while holding up an instrument that looked like pliers but had some kind of bolt going through the handles joining them. *'I designed the changes my self — much more efficient now.'* He had taken each of her mother's fingers, put the pliers around the knuckles and slowly tightened the screw to increase the pressure on the bones. Catherine remembers her mums face, her eyes bloodshot and crying while her screams, stifled by the duct-tape, were still terrible to hear; as was the ugly popping of bone when the pliers finally crushed the knuckle.

How could Logan think she would ever forget a man like that? His voice has haunted her over the years — she can hear it still.

"Catherine," Logan smiles looking somewhat relieved, "I've been searching the house for you." *And so the sun shines in my world again.*

"Sorry," she smiles back, having missed him more than she realised, "locked out." Catherine explains about lunch with Ben. "He was a bit off at first," she recalls, "probably annoyed by the fact that I'm still not going into the office; and he has a point."

*Because I'm a selfish cow, only ever thinking about me. Sorry, mum.*

"Have you ever considered making him a partner?" Logan asks while taking a seat beside Catherine. She looks shocked and bemused at the suggestion. "I'll take that as a no," he chuckles then draws her in for a long tender kiss. "Mmm," he sighs as their lips reluctantly part, "I've been looking forward to doing that all day." *Wow! Don't stop on my account.*

Leaving his arm around her shoulders, Catherine snuggles in. "I...missed you too," she confesses shyly; then hurriedly changes the subject. "Don't you have to train to play rugby? I mean, are you not doing things that you normally would because I'm staying here?"

Putting a finger under her chin, Logan draws her face up to look at him and watches her blush prettily. "You are not in the way of anything important," he assures Catherine, then bends to kiss the tip of her nose. "I spoke to Carl, the team captain, yesterday and explained that I won't be free for at least a couple of weeks." She wants to protest, to be unselfish enough to tell him he should go, but the memories of her mum and what that man did to her prevent Catherine.

Logan can see the conflict of emotions play out on Catherine's unguarded expression. "What we are doing now is more important than rugby, my work or yours," he tells her gently but firmly. "Part of the reason I had to go in today was to set things up so that they could run without me, for the most part, for at least the next few weeks."

"I'm so lucky to have you in my corner," she sighs and moves her head back to lean against his lovely broad shoulder.

"In your corner, in your life," he tells her simply, "for as long as you'll have me." *I wish I could believe that. I want to believe...*

They take a companionable walk around the garden before heading indoors to resume their task.

"I've got a spare front door key hanging in the kitchen," he tells her once they are inside. "I'll get it for you now and bring a jug of coffee in – I think we're going to need it."

They do. By midnight, the second jug of coffee is gone, their heads are aching but Catherine has found a break at last. "Logan, look at this," she calls over excitedly.

Leaning in to look over her shoulder, Logan is astounded by what he reads. "Good lord, it could be a mirror image of what happened to your mother," he gasps. "I wonder if the police have put the two together – it can't be a coincidence, opposite ends of the country maybe, but it must be the same man!"

Catherine agrees, feeling that at last they are getting somewhere.

*We're closing in, and when we find you I'll...*

The following morning they sit having breakfast together in the conservatory, looking out at another lovely day.

"You should inform the police of what you found last night," Logan tells her as he watches Catherine nibble on a slice of toast. "Even if they have made the connection, it won't hurt to let them know you're still looking for answers."

"Do you think they even care?" she asks. "It's not like my mum was anyone important; not to anyone else, anyway." *I miss you so much.*

He reaches across and takes her hand. "Your mum was, is, as important as any other murder victim. No doubt the police have spoken to hundreds of people and followed numerous clues; but you may have made a connection that they haven't yet." He gives her hand a squeeze then lets it go.

"Maybe," she agrees, "I just don't want to get my hopes up. Finding this other victim could be a huge break, but if they've already connected the two its nothing more than another case to add to our growing spreadsheet."

She is right, he knows, but Logan wants, so much, to wipe the dejection from her eyes and see them sparkle with life again. "Right you are," he agrees, pushing his chair back to stand. "Come on then, let's find out instead of sitting here speculating." He holds out a hand towards Catherine and she takes it reluctantly. "It's better to know one way or the other," he assures her as they make their way to the lounge. "If you want privacy I can wait for you back in the conservatory," he offers, but Catherine is already shaking her head.

"Stay, please," she tells him, then circles her arms around his waist and just clings on to his strength. "I need you to."

His arms fold around her lovingly, protectively. "Then I will." He lays his cheek on the top of her head then lifts it to place a kiss there. "Let's get this done." With that, he guides her over to the window chair next to the telephone and she sits down to make the call.

*Please, please, please...please let this be a good lead.*

Picking up the phone, Catherine's hand trembles as she punches in the number for the operator and asks to be put through to the Sheriton Police Station. "Yes, hello," she replies to the desk officer's offer of help, "I want to speak to Inspector Harper; it's about a murder case he was investigating fifteen years ago." *What if he's retired? What if he's dead?* Catherine was put on hold and looks over at Logan for support while she waits. "Yes I do," she replies when the Inspector asks if she has some information for him. *Oh, thank the gods he's alive!* "It's about the Sara Colson murder; I'm her daughter, Catherine." She listens to him tapping computer keys to bring up her mother's file. Then the line goes silent for a while and she assumes he is refreshing himself on the facts.

"Christ!" She hears him blow out wearily, and then answers all the questions he asks of her. "So you think this might be a useful lead?" she asks and smiles over at Logan hopefully. "Thank you inspector, you can contact me on that mobile number I just gave you twenty-four-seven."

*At last!*

Putting the phone down, Catherine shoots her arms up in the air and shouts, "Yes!"

Logan swings her up and around in the air while Catherine laughs like a loon. Sliding her down his body Logan hugs her tight then kisses her so gently. He wants nothing more than to love her, to show her some unconditional tenderness.

She is smiling now, her brilliant blue eyes dancing with excitement. "I need to go home," she tells him. Logan looks bemused and disappointed and Catherine laughs. "My phone is dead – I need to get my charger. God knows how many messages are on it after all this time."

His smile back in place, Logan gets his car keys to take her immediately. "You can pick up a few more things, if you need them, too."

Catherine looks over at him, wondering why he appears to want her to stay. It's not like he's even getting sex for his trouble – Logan seems to have gone off the idea. "I could move back home and just come over for a few hours to work on the computer each day," she offers, not sure how she feels about the idea herself; and is glad when Logan dismisses it out of hand.

"Not a lot of sense in that," he tells her, ushering Catherine out of the front door. "We'll definitely get a lot more done if you're already here. And besides," he tickles her side playfully, laughing when she squeals and jumps to one side, "I've gotten used to having you around." *Me too.*

When they reach Catherine's house, where her bedsit awaits her return, Logan looks up at it curiously. "Why haven't you ever moved out into your own place?" "Because this is my own place," she replies still smiling.

"It's the first home I ever lived in where the only key to my very own space is mine, and I'm hardly there most of the time. It's really just a place to crash and change." *But it's my place.*

"Then you don't miss it?" he asks. "When you're at mine," he clarifies when she frowns.

Catherine's mind goes into a spin – how is she supposed to answer a loaded question like that? If she says yes, she does then Logan might think she isn't happy spending time with him, when she is. More than happy! But if she says no, she doesn't then he might think she is being pushy, maybe even wanting to move in with him.

*Mmm!*

Before she can answer, Logan laughs. "It isn't a trick question, Catherine. I just wondered, that's all. Now, let's get your things and get back to work."

She knows the work he's referring to and is as keen as he to get back to it.

Catherine pulls a couple of pairs of tracky bottoms out of her wardrobe and receives a disapproving frown from Logan. "I'm not going to live in them," she tells him, "and I'll even wear them with one of those fancy tops you got me to buy; but they are comfortable for round the house."

"I'll hold you to that," his lovely dark voice isn't even slightly threatening, and her smile tells him so. "I mean it," he wags a warning finger at her, "in the house only. You look too lovely in your new clothes to go back to wearing those." *Nice to know, Mr Sayers. Nice to know.*

"Yes boss," she laughs, and moves to collect her laptop and her phone charger. "Ok, that should do it," she tells him, picking up her car keys and moving towards the door.

"What do you need those for?" Logan points to the car keys in her hand, "I can take you anywhere you need to go."

But Catherine needs her independence, even if it is only in this small way. "Ok, so what if your office needs you to go in at the same time as mine does? We both still have businesses to run, Logan, which is why I'm also bringing this," and she holds up the arm that has her laptop tucked under it.

He knows she is right, but Logan enjoys doing things together. However, he realises that he has to give her more room or risk ruining their relationship. "Ok, you win," and his smile is firmly back in place. "But I wish you'd invest in a new car; yours looks to be on its last legs." *Hey! Don't knock the car!*

When they get to the street, Catherine looks at her car affectionately. "I know you're right," she admits, her hand trailing lovingly over her old Fiesta's bonnet, "but this is my first car, and she's never let me down." However, she declines to tell him how many times it has been a close thing. Like on the day she met him for the first time at Arthur Kingsley's office – she had been begging the car to start that morning, and luckily, it had, eventually. "I suppose your first car was a Porsche," she states crossly. *And I bet you didn't pay for it!*

He is used to her taciturn moods by now and knows she is just being defensive. "Not a chance," he smiles as she turns to look at him. "My parents weren't born well off, they had to earn it the same as most others. So, being very pragmatic about the expected bumps in the first year, they bought me an old, two door Maestro. It was brilliant," he enthuses as she brightens considerably, "my mates and I used to go out cruising just for the sake of it half the time."

"Picking up babes," she frowns, but gives him a crooked smile. "You tart! I bet you were putting yourself about like a regular Don Juan." They both laugh at that.

Catherine sobers first and tells him what she has been thinking about doing. "What you said made sense," she tells him agreeably. "It just didn't occur to me before."

Logan nods. "You don't have to offer him an even partnership," he explains knowledgeably, "you could keep a controlling interest and offer Ben, say, thirty to forty percent – according to how much you value his worth to the company."

"He is a terrific asset," she confirms. "I'd be hard pushed to replace him." *Who knows what dross is out there. And we're friends. We work well together.*

"Give it some thought," he encourages, walking her to the driver's door of her car, "I'll follow you back to make sure you don't break down on the way." He is smiling teasingly, but Catherine just sticks her tongue out at Logan making him laugh.

"I think I'll go into the office and discuss this with Ben now," she tells him, feeling nervous for some reason.

"Fine, I'll see you back at the house later." He gives her a wave then climbs into his car waiting for Catherine to pull away. He does follow behind her, until they reached the junction where she needs to turn off and he gives her a pip on the horn as he continues on his way.

Pulling her car into the spot next to Ben's sports car, Catherine gets out and compares them ruefully. Perhaps Logan is right; she winces at the gleaming exterior of Ben's sporty Saab and the dull shabbiness of her Fiesta.

*Well*, she thinks, making towards the outer office door, *that will have to be a problem for another day.*

It is cooler in the tiny corridor, which leads to the two offices and a small kitchenette, and she can hear Ben hard at work. *Yes*, she confirms in her own mind, *he's well worth forty percent of anyone's money*, and moves to his open office door.

"Hard at it, I see." Ben jumps a mile in the air at the unexpected sound of her voice. She knows she shouldn't but she can't help laughing. "Bloody hell, Ben," she watches him clutch at his heart and drag in a couple of sharp breathes, "with nerves like that it's a wonder you haven't had a heart attack before now!"

He is smiling now and really pleased to see her. "With a boss like you I'll no doubt get around to having one; just give it time," he tells her with a sarcastic grin.

"Actually, Ben, that's sort of what I came in to talk to you about," then draws up his visitors chair to sit opposite him.

"You've come to talk to me about my heart," he jokes, "how very touching."

Deciding not to sit after all, Catherine gets to her feet and starts to pace. "You and I," she starts hesitantly, "we've worked well together for a long time now." Ben nods silently. "And, even more than that, we're friends," she states, and watches him nod again. "Well...that being the case...I don't see any reason why we can't be more than friends," she offers, and is pleased to see him smile broadly, but before she can finish Ben leaps out of his chair and kisses her. Stunned, Catherine is bereft of speech. *What the fuck!*

"You don't know how happy you've just made me," Ben hugs her again. "I've been waiting all this time for the right moment, and here you are beating me to it." He makes to kiss her again, but Catherine has started to come to her senses. *Where the hell did this come from?*

"Ben, stop!" Putting her hands against his chest, she looks at him incredulously. "I had no idea you felt that way." Catherine takes a step back to emphasise her words. "Did I do something to encourage you...or...or...to make you think I felt the same way?" she stammers. *Not again! What did I do this time?*

"But you just said...?" It is Ben's turn to look confused; and hurt Catherine realises. *Oh, Ben...I'm such a fool!*

"I was talking about the business, Ben," she tries to explain, and watches him sit heavily back down. "I'm so sorry – I was offering you a partnership, only I seem to have made a royal mess of it." Catherine sits down too, watching her friend of the last six years go from ecstatic joy to crushed hurt in short order. *Shit!*

Ben stands up and leaves the office. She hears him pottering about in the kitchen and waits for his return. When he does he looks angry, but has taken the time to make two mugs of tea. "I should have known," his voice is bitter and sharp as he hands her a mug, "it's that rich bastard, Sayers, right?"

Catherine nods and watches the dagger slide home. Ben's face twists with the pain of her acknowledgement. "I can give you everything that he can," he tells her proudly. "More, probably, as we have so much in common – I mean, who knows you better than I do? Who understands your love of this business better than me?" He prods a finger hard into his own chest. "I've loved you right from the beginning – why do you think I've been so willing to put up with your quirks and tantrums?" he tells her more gently, actually managing the ghost of a smile. "I love you, Catherine, and now that you know maybe the idea will grow on you," he continues hopefully. *Oh, Ben.*

"I should go." Catherine stands abruptly, turning for the door, stopping just short of stepping through it. "I would never hurt you deliberately," she tells him, and turns moist eyes to look at Ben, "you know that, right?"

He nods wordlessly, not making any attempt to stop her from leaving.

She cries all the way to Logan's house; confused and full of self-loathing, Catherine is devastated. *What a bitch! What a god-damned awful bitch!*

Logan finds her; forehead leaning against the steering wheel, still crying her heart out. "Come on," he encourages, a hand under her arm to help her out of the car, "you look like you could use a stiff drink."

Catherine allows him to steer her inside the house and sit her down in the lounge where he pours her a Brandy. "Drink that down," he orders softly, "it'll put some colour back in your cheeks."

She sips and grimaces then does as she's been told. "Yuk! Whatever the fuck that is I don't want any more!" she frowns deeply and shudders.

"And she's back," Logan laughs then moves forward, sitting on his haunches to look at her. "Want to tell me about it?"

Her head falls forward onto his shoulder and her arms go round his neck. "I'm a terrible, loathsome person," she declares. "I should be shot at the earliest opportunity."

"I'll kill any man who tries," Logan declares dramatically, and feels the smile he wanted reluctantly tug at her lips. "Now tell me why you should be shot and maybe I'll oblige."

She sits up then and studies him, even the reluctant smile struggling to stay in place. "Ben's in love with me," Catherine blurts out, still amazed at the discovery. "Can you believe it?" she asks wide-eyed and completely innocent.

"Yes, I can." He reaches a hand up to stroke the soft waves of her growing hair. "You don't see yourself as others do," he tells her. "I watched the other guests when you arrived at Robert's party – the women were jealous and the men were lusting after you." His brown eyes grow molten with the memory. "And I was just as bad," he admits honestly. Her head tilts to one side, and Catherine has to wonder just how stupid she really is – yet again, she'd had no idea. "Then when I took you home and had the privilege of undressing you and putting you to bed, I fell deeply, madly in lust with you." He laughs at himself and Catherine punches his shoulder none too gently. *Huh!*

"Yeah, right," she scorns, rolling her eyes at him, "that's why you haven't touched me since we got back from Lakelands." Then she blushes as she realises what she has said. *Nice one! Way to go, Catherine!*

"You silly goose." He puts a hand to her hot cheeks and studies her. "I haven't touched you because we've been busy and you've been upset – understandably so," he tells her. Then decides it's a good time to come completely clean. "Catherine, I had an idea about Ben," Logan confesses, and when she straightens in surprise he has to strengthen his resolve to be honest no matter what it costs him. "I didn't expect what happened today, but I did think it would happen sooner or later."

Her eyes widen as Catherine shakes her head and stares at him. "I really don't get it – I've worked with the man closely over the last six years and didn't get an inkling – you've known him for all of five bloody minutes and his hearts an open book. What the fuck...?" she asks the heavens, her hands lifting palms up and her eyes going up to look at the ceiling. *Give me a clue here!*

"I think that was the problem," he consoles her; "you were too close to see what was going on. No doubt if you had been in my shoes you would have come to the same conclusion." *I wouldn't bet on it! Shit!*

"So why didn't you give me a heads up?" she asks, still feeling annoyed, and more than a little stupid. "It might have helped going in if I'd known what I was walking in to," she chides.

Logan looks at the floor for a long moment, and then lets it all pour out. "I didn't tell you because I wanted to give Ben his chance." When Catherine makes to comment, Logan holds up a staying hand. "Just listen to me, a minute," he asks getting to his feet and walking to stand by the fireplace. "I'm thirty six and you're twenty five – ok, nearly twenty six," he concedes when again she makes to interrupt. "That still makes me ten years older than you, and you deserve better," he finishes quietly, turning to stare into the empty grate, his insides feeling just as dead as the ashes he sees there, at the thought of living without her.

"I know I'm stupid about this relationship lark," she stands angrily, "but are you really telling me that I'm not allowed to love you because you happen to be older than I am? *What a crock of shit! Jesus, and I thought I was thick!*

It is music to his ears and his heart barely dares to hope. "Be very careful how you answer this next question," he tells Catherine softly, moving to stand in front of her. "Did you just say that you love me?" His heart is beating wildly then explodes with joy when she nods shyly. "You wonderful woman," he laughs; swinging her round until she laughingly begs him to stop. Logan slides her down his body then holds her to him as if he would never let her go. "I love you, Catherine Colson," he declares earnestly, quietly, "and I'll never let anyone hurt you again for as long as we live." *Bliss. Pure bliss.*

Reaching her arms up she pulls his head down to taste his lips; something she has been dying to do properly for what seems the longest time. They move into the kiss, deepening it as their love flows freely between them for the first time.

"I want you desperately, Catherine," Logan tells her, his need for her so strong he has to fight it down, "let me take you to bed?" *Touché!*

They both smile, remembering when Catherine uttered that same invitation to him at Lakelands. She nods again, her smile teasing, "I promise not to faint this time."

He scoops her up into his arms, not a hint of strain in his muscular body as he carries her up the stairs to his bedroom. Logan lowers her to her feet and regards Catherine soberly. "I'm going to repeat what I said to you at Lakelands," he begins, tracing a gentle finger down her cheek, "if you want me to stop, at any time, I will." *Don't you dare!*

Catherine doesn't doubt that he means it, but nothing short of an earthquake will stop her from having him now. "Not a chance," she growls, her needs already making themselves known. Lifting her dress over her head, Catherine throws it on the floor and stands in just her underwear longing for that first touch; but first she has to get them on an even footing, and tugs at the buttons of his shirt with unsteady hands.

Logan actually laughs, then takes pity and helps her. "You'll have to get more practice," he jiggles his eyebrows suggestively after throwing his shirt down on top of her dress on the floor.

However, Catherine is more interested in the broad expanse of chest he's bared for her, and moving to him places one palm against his racing heart, her other at the back of his neck to lower his head.

When their lips meet, there is no hesitation. The heat that fires in one only serves to fuel the other. As gentle as Logan tries to be, Catherine is determined to give as well as receive this time. She might be a virgin, but she knows, more or less, what's what and wants to please this wonderful man who loves her. *My own wonderful, unbelievable miracle.*

Managing to undo his trousers, Catherine jerks them down and Logan steps out of them. Before he knows what she plans to do, Catherine drops to her knees and tugging him free, takes him into her mouth. Logan's head flings back, a deep groan of pleasure and restraint roaring out of him as Catherine works him hard. Her instincts are to give, and she does so, loving his response to her touch, feeling the heady thrill of her power over him.

"Catherine, please," Logan moves back, pulling her to her feet, before his restraint fails, "I want to make love to you and I won't manage that if you send me over the edge too soon." He kisses her gently, pulling her back into his arms, allowing their passions to level out for now. He lifts her then, climbing on to the bed and laying her down beneath him. Looking in to her diamond bright eyes he sees no fear – sure, now, that she is ready to take this next step. He feels the wet heat of her when he reaches down to cup her, then Catherine's eyelids flutter closed and her breath catches when his fingers slide under her panties and inside her. She groans helplessly as his deft fingers and agile thumb work their wonderful magic, taking her so high she is giddy with it.

The fall, when it comes, is like tumbling from a great height and she screams with the ferocity of it.

Logan removes her underwear and his own, and then moves to take her firm breasts in his hands, lowering his mouth to taste her. His teeth rake over her nipples then his tongue licks over the sensitised flesh, and Catherine feels the heat in her loins growing again, arching her back as the pleasure surges through her. "Again, Catherine," he urges eagerly, moving down her body to feed hungrily on the heat of her sex.

When she feels his tongue exploring her inside and out, Catherine clutches at the bedding to steady herself but her world rocks violently as she soars even higher than before; then begins that wonderful fall as she crests over the edge of heaven. *Yes! Yes! Holy shit! Yes!*

Logan moves to lie beside Catherine, stroking her damp hair back from her beautiful face. "You're amazing," he says, leaning up on one elbow to smile down at her.

*And...*

She looks up at Logan, barely able to speak, lifts her hand to his cheek and says, "I love you." He bends his head and the kiss that follows is long and deep. "I want all of you," she tells him, watching Logan steadily; but he seems to be backing away. "I won't stay a virgin forever," she states, knowing it is this that is holding him back. She pulls his head down to kiss him, her other hand reaching down to grasp and pleasure him as he had her. Then she takes him completely off guard, flips him on to his back and impales herself upon him.

Her body erupts on an orgasm that tears right through her, and Logan is dragged over the edge with the strength of it as she clamps fiercely around him.  They cry out in unison then Catherine falls into his arms as Logan pulls her to him.

She is his now, and he is hers, and the rest of the world be damned if they don't approve.

# Chapter Seven

Logan stands in the doorway of his kitchen unnoticed, watching Catherine pad about in bare feet and wearing one of his shirts. Not that he minds, he thinks she looks better in it than he does – especially the way she is jiggling about to the music. "You look happy," he tells her, then laughs when she jumps and almost drops her toast.

He walks over; puts his arms around her waist while she reaches up and crosses hers at the back of his neck. "You were supposed to stay in bed," she rebukes him playfully. "I was going to make some tea and toast and bring it up."

"Nice thought," he grins, "we can have it in the conservatory instead."

They both stand with heads jerked up and ears listening to the ring of a mobile phone. "Mine," Catherine says before planting a swift kiss on his lips then running off into the lounge. "Hello," she answers, fumbling between her toast and the phone. "Oh, thank you for getting back to me so quickly. Could you wait for just a moment," crossing to the door she waves for Logan to come and join her, "I'm putting the phone on speaker so that Mr Sayers, Logan, can hear you too – he's been a great help with research on the computer."

"That's fine, the more input we can get the better," they both hear Inspector Harper reply. "Now, I wanted to talk to you about your concerns regarding a Mr Charles Llwyd – you seem very sure that you remember his voice specifically, why is that Ms Colson?"

"The man who attacked my mum spoke constantly, telling me everything he was about to do before he did it," Catherine explains, "and you don't forget a voice like that. I still have nightmares about it."

"Recently?" the Inspector asks.

Logan, too, looks interested in her answer.

"Yes," she admits quietly, "worse since all this started up again."

The Inspector's reply is a low, "Mmm," and Logan takes her hand in support.

"You think I'm cracking up," she accuses, rubbing her free hand across her eyes. "Are you taking anything I've said seriously, or is this just a, placate and side-line call?"

They hear the Inspector clear his throat, "I most certainly am taking you seriously," he insists. "That is why I needed to check just how sure you are – we will be following this lead up very closely if you are certain that Mr Llwyd's voice is at least a close match to the perpetrator of these hideous crimes."

Catherine says, "I'm very certain."

Then Logan says, "You said, 'crimes', Inspector – does that mean you have made a positive connection between the murders of Sara Colson and Harriet Leavesden?"

The Inspector seems to hesitate. "We have," he confirms, "but I must ask you to keep that information strictly between yourselves. We don't want to show our hand to the perpetrator; if he thinks we're getting close he could run and his trail go completely cold."

"No problem, Inspector," Catherine confirms; and Logan adds, "Absolutely."

"Good, then I'll get on and liaise with the Moorsden Police Force," Inspector Harper informs them. "Can't say too much, but I can assure you, Ms Colson, the wheels are very much in motion."

Catherine thanks the Inspector, and when he has gone turns into Logan.

"I can hardly bare to hope," she mumbles into his chest, "but it really is a good lead, isn't it?"

"The best you could hope for," Logan encourages, his strong arms enfolding Catherine, wanting to shield her from hurt.

Turning her face up to him, she smiles suggestively. "You know...you could always take my mind off things for a while." Her fingers start undoing his shirt buttons and Logan laughs. "Well, you did say I need to practice," she chuckles as she finishes with the buttons and draws his shirt off, then sighs in admiration of his wonderful physique. *What a body, and its all mine.*

Her hands trail over Logan's muscular arms, her eyes watching for his reaction. Then she trails her fingers over his broad chest and through the curling mass of hair following it down past his navel to the waistband of his slacks. Popping the fastener, Catherine draws the zip down slowly, watching her man tense as her hand finds its way inside his fly and rubs along his hard length through his boxers. Logan's breathing hitches as she gives him a gentle squeeze before divesting him of his trousers.

Catherine is still only wearing his shirt, so Logan's work is short. "You should wear my shirts more often," he tells her, taking her full breasts in his hands, flicking his thumbs over their tips, her response a sharp intake of breath. "How lovely you are," his lips trail up her neck to find her ear lobes. When his teeth and tongue tease and explore, Catherine finds herself holding onto him for support. "Just let yourself experience each sensation," he moves round the back of her, kissing her nape his hands reaching forward first to cup her breasts then moving slowly downward. As his fingers delve into her wet heat, Catherine cries out her head falling back. Cresting over the first peak quickly, her knees buckle beneath her. Logan catches her up then lowers them both to the floor. Removing the rest of his clothes, he moves over Catherine and enters her slowly.

"Oh god," she breathes as his slow drawn out rhythm drives her up again. His hands slide beneath her buttocks lifting her hips off the floor. Then she feels the hard length of him drive even further into her, filling her, and only begs for more. "Don't stop...don't stop." The speed of his rhythm increases and the depths he plumbs are so amazingly sensitive. "Logan..." her hands hold on to his arms and she looks up to see his pleasure and his love, "...together...now." Still looking into each other's eyes, they crest the last wave as one; their bodies united their voices crying out in a sensual duet.

They lie sated and exhausted, holding each other. Catherine's head lies against Logan's chest and he lifts his head to place a kiss on the top of hers. "Are you ok?" he asks, concerned that she might still be tender as the previous night had been Catherine's first experience with any man. "Did I hurt you?"

She laughs, moving her hand gently over his still heaving chest. "Are you kidding," she turns her face into him and kissed his nipple, "I have never felt better. In fact, I can't believe what I've been missing," raising her head up she smiles lustily her eyes travelling down his body all but devouring him. When her eyes come back to his, she finds their brown depths molten; he wants her as much as she needs him. Only this time she wants to explore his body and gauge his responses.

"Turn over," Catherine tells him. When he is on his stomach, she uses her hands to caress muscles that quiver expectantly. Replacing her hands with her lips Catherine kisses the nape of his neck as he had done to her and feels him respond in a way she recognises and smiles with satisfaction. Then she straddles his back and leaning forward uses her lips and teeth on his ear just as he had to her, and again gets a very satisfactory response.

"You learn fast," the tremor in his voice expressing his growing need better than any words.

Catherine chuckles enjoying her new-found power. "I want to learn more," and she moves her lips and tongue over his shoulders tasting the maleness of his skin. Her mouth and hands explore every dip and hollow, lingering over the hard muscle beneath. When she reaches his taught buttocks, she feels them tense and uses her teeth to nip at them playfully.

"Catherine, you're killing me," he groans, toppling her as he rolls onto his back. When he makes to move atop her, Catherine puts up a hand to stop him.

Her cheeks aglow and her smile nervous Catherine asks, "Show me how, teach me to be the one on top."

Rolling on to his back again, Logan pulls her with him so that Catherine now sits astride him. "When you're ready, just guide me in and feel the new sensations then move however pleases you," he encourages.

She looks down; he looks bigger and harder than ever from this angle. "Will it hurt?" she asks, moving her hands over the length of him.

Logan shakes his head. "No, you have full control," he assures her, "depth speed and rhythm are all up to you." He lets out a groan, her fingers working him gently.

She is already hot and wet so entry is no problem, but she is nervous of the size of him so only slides a little way down before moving back up. Catherine places her hands either side of his head, her breasts falling just right for his mouth to reach and she groans when he tastes and rolls their tips between his lips and teeth. Catherine starts slow then, as her needs grow, she moves faster taking more of him inside. She doesn't need to ask him if she is doing it right, his breathing is as ragged as hers. The slow boil in her loins is making its way up her body demanding to be satisfied. As the crescendo builds she pushes back hard, taking him fully inside and sitting upright rocks her hips without thought, just following the rhythm of her need.

Logan groans as he feels her tighten around him and topples with her off the edge of the world.

This time they lay silent and spent, content just to lie in each other's arms. Their hearts are hammering and their breathing laboured, but both are smiling foolishly.

"It's a good job Mrs Baines isn't due in today," Logan observes, and clamps his arm over Catherine when she makes to jump up. "I don't know when I'll be able to stand again, let alone walk," he laughs softly.

"Bloody hell," she gasps, "I completely forgot all about her – what if she'd walked in on us. I'd never be able to show my face again," and she blushes deeply at the awful thought.

Logan eases them both up to sit leaning their backs against the settee. "I'll race you for the shower,"

Catherine challenges, then reaches over for the shirt she had been wearing earlier and pulls it on.

Grabbing his clothes up, Logan follows behind her then scoops her off her feet when they reach the top of the stairs. Catherine is laughing and kicking, "You brute...that's cheating," but he holds on to her until they are in the bedroom.

"Being as I'm such a gentleman," he laughs as she wriggles and squirms in his arms, "I'll let you use the shower first, just this once. Then, I suggest we get back to work – we found one other victim, who's to say there aren't more."   Letting her feet slide back to the floor, Logan manages to side step a swipe at his bottom.

Catherine is working on her laptop – it is top of the line and she has made some of her own adjustments to give it more speed and abilities. If she had wanted to she could have made a good career in computers, designing building and programming come easily to Catherine. For now, though, she is putting her considerable skills to work on finding her mum's murderer; determined to stop his reign of terror.

Getting up to pour another mug of coffee, Catherine moves over to Logan first. "I'm going to get some more coffee, do you want some?" she asks.

His computer screen changes before she gets near enough to see it and Logan nods his head. "That'd be great," he yawns before he can stifle it, "then maybe we should call it a night."

Bringing a mug of hot coffee over to him, Catherine takes a sip of her own then shakes her head. "I'm good for another couple of hours, but you go up," she tells him, "I don't mind."

Logan's back straightens. "I can manage another couple of hours," he states firmly. "I just thought you might like to get some sleep and come at it fresh in the morning."

Smiling, realising that she has touched a nerve, Catherine crosses to kiss him. "I'm tired too," she tells Logan, and does indeed have to smother a yawn, "but I think I may be on to something and want to keep going while my thoughts are on track."

"What is it?" he frowns up at her. "Have you found another victim?"

"I'm not sure what I've found, or if I've found anything," she replies cryptically. "I just want a chance to work this through a bit longer and then we'll go up."

He nods and Catherine moves to retake her seat and buries her head back in her computer. Logan also goes back to work – he has some decent computer skills and has used them to find Catherine's father. Maybe she doesn't want to know who or where he is, but Logan is curious and thought he would save the information until she is ready to hear it – but he has hit a snag; a big one.

The snag is named Caroline Thornton, a gifted pianist she is currently touring Europe with her father Thomas Thornton. In approximately six weeks, on July 15th, she will be twenty-six years old, the exact same age as Catherine, her twin sister.

Mrs Baines serves breakfast in the conservatory the next morning. "Are you sure you don't want some more, dearie?" eyeing Catherine's slender frame it is obvious that the rotund housekeeper thinks she needs feeding up.

With a hand to her well-filled stomach, Catherine declines politely. "That has to be one of the best breakfasts I've had in a while," she beams at the housekeeper then turns her eyes on Logan. "In fact, I'd have to say that it comes in neck and neck with your father's cooking – and that was bloody brilliant," she confirms to both of them.

"If that bacon is going begging," Logan eyes the warming plate that the housekeeper is about to take away, "I wouldn't say no to another helping."

Mrs Baines thrusts her impressive chest out proudly. "Always a pleasure to cook for a man who enjoys his food." Emptying the last of the bacon onto Logan's plate, she moves off into the kitchen.

Catherine watches as Logan devours his second helping of bacon then smiles teasingly. "You know, with you not playing rugby at the moment, and not going into work either, you might need to watch your waistline."

Almost spluttering on his last mouthful, Logan swallows manfully. "There's nothing wrong with my waistline," Logan sits up even straighter, patting a hand against a firm wall of muscle that forms his abdomen. "Though I must admit, I could use a workout in the gym – it seems I've been a bit distracted from my usual routine, of late." His voice and smile are playfully rebuking, and then openly loving. "But I wouldn't have it any other way," he reaches across the table to pick up her hand and brings it to his lips.

Catherine pulls it sharply back, her cheeks reddening as Mrs Baines brings a tray of coffee into the conservatory. "Thank you, Mrs Baines, would you mind closing the doors on your way out," Logan smiles. He waits until the housekeeper has gone, then turns serious eyes to Catherine. "I think it's time to bring each other up to date on our progress. You've been looking at some kind of new lead, I think you said?"

She is suddenly animated, sitting forward in her seat and hotching it over to move nearer to Logan. "I've been searching the police databases for the injuries inflicted rather than the whole profile of injuries and attack pattern," Catherine tells him excitedly. Then, watching as Logan pales she adds," Don't worry, I've done it loads of times, and I made sure to use my own laptop – I'm sure your security is fine but mine is top of the line; my line that is," she clarifies.

"You've been hacking into police records," he frowns, his face now full of concern, "do you have any idea of the trouble you could get in if they even suspect that's what you've been doing?"

She waves his concern aside. "I'm not stupid, I'm careful not to leave traces – there is no way they can trace any activity back to me. In fact, I'm damn sure they have no idea anyone has been looking through their records; I wrote the program I use to get in and out myself."

Logan still looks concerned, but smiles resignedly. "Well, I hope whatever you found is worth the risks you took?"

Sitting back in her chair, Catherine looks pleased with herself. "I went back twenty-five years," she begins, finishing her coffee and placing the cup back on the table, "and I looked for any kind of injury that would take some kind of implement to inflict." Sitting forward in her seat again, her eyes take on a brilliant blue light of excitement. "I found loads; young boys with their knuckles crushed, or their nails pulled out or some kind of heated needle pushed up underneath them." She watches Logan grimace. "I know; there were some seriously gruesome injuries depicted with photographic documentation. I swear, Logan, some of those photos could have been of my mum's injuries. They were carbon copies," she finishes, waiting expectantly for his opinion.

"So, you're thinking these could be practice attacks prior to moving on to actual murder?" he asks, then continues when she nods. "And you found the first sign of this type of injury when?"

"Twenty-three years back," she smiles then her eyes take on a determined gleam. "They started out in a small cluster," she states then watches as the penny begins to drop for Logan. "Glywyth in Wales, which ties right in with the Welsh accent my mother's murderer had," her chin lifts defiantly, triumphantly, "and the Welsh accent that your friend, Mr Charles Llwyd, still has to this day."

They watch each other in silence, Catherine leaning over to the coffee filter jug to top up both their cups. Picking hers up, she says, "So...no comments?"

Picking his cup up, Logan drinks thoughtfully before putting it back down on the table. "Actually, I think this might be an opportune moment to bring you up to date with my own findings," he tells Catherine and watches her expression shift to one of suspicion. "I've been doing a bit of deep digging of my own," he states cautiously. "As you know, I've had dealings with Charles for quite a number of years, as has Arthur Kingsley." Catherine nods her agreement. "I checked back in my own records to see if we were dealing with Charles around the time of both murders. It turned out that we were not, but when I checked with Arthur he told me that he was dealing with Charles just after the time when Harriet Leavesden was murdered."

"But that doesn't tell us anything," Catherine states hotly, annoyed that her findings are being so easily dismissed.

"No, you're right," Logan holds up a hand of peace, "but the reason Arthur dealt with Charles after the date when Harriet Leavesden was murdered is because Charles was out of the country. He flew back three days after her death, having been in Australia for almost a month." Logan watches the effects of his words on Catherine, first abject disbelief then reluctant contemplation as she tries to put the jigsaw of facts together to form a different picture.

"I was so sure...," her head shaking slowly as if in denial, "...I mean, you have to admit, the coincidence is hard to believe."

"I do agree, the coincidence is staggering," Logan reaches across to take Catherine's hand again, "but the facts are undeniable and concrete." Watching her eyes close on a heavy sigh, Logan is loath to add to her misery. "Catherine, I have something else I need to discuss with you," he tells her gently then waits until her eyes open to regard him. "It has nothing to do with the murders," he tells her quickly then gives her hand a squeeze and takes a bracing breath. "I've found your father," he informs her bluntly.

Shooting to her feet Catherine snatches her hand out of his and stares daggers into Logan. "What the fuck do you mean, you've found my father?"

"I didn't mean to look," Logan begins uncertainly, "but I found myself wondering. You have grown up thinking you have no one. You've clawed your way to the top of a very competitive business and have never had anyone to share that success with. No one to say well done, I'm proud of you." He sighs deeply when she remains stiff and unmoving. "Catherine, if I'd found out he is a waster, a user, then I'd never have told you about him –"

She cuts him off abruptly. "I beg your pardon!" It isn't a question, but a rebuke spoken so deathly quiet that an icy chill hangs in the air between them.

"I just meant...I know how reluctant you've been to know anything about your father; if I'd come across something hurtful then naturally I'd have spared you that." Logan knows he is digging a hole for himself and no matter what he says Catherine will bury him in it if he isn't careful.

"So, you get to know all my darkest secrets," Catherine sneers down at Logan, her face a picture of utter contempt, "and then you get to decide just what you'll let me know. What you think is good for me," her voice remains quiet but the ice in it is freezing fast.

"That isn't what I meant at all." Logan stands, his impressive height and build not intimidating Catherine in the least. "You're twisting what I said and deliberately misunderstanding my intent." His hands rise then fall in front of him, "All I want is to protect your feelings."

"You trampled all over them the minute you went behind my back." Catherine turns, striding angrily towards the conservatory door.

"You have a sister," Logan shoots out, stopping Catherine dead in her tracks. When she turns back to face him all colour has gone from her cheeks. "You have a sister," he repeats more softly, "her name is Caroline Thornton and she will be twenty-six on the fifteenth of July."

Catherine feels light-headed and reaches out a hand to the back of a chair to steady her. "A sister...," she frowns, her mind whirling, "...a twin sister?"

"Yes," Logan confirms, wanting to go to her but knowing Catherine will not allow it.

Pulling the chair out from the table Catherine slumps down onto it. "That's enough," she breathes, trying desperately to pull herself together, and when she thinks she has, Catherine looks up at Logan her blue eyes cold as steel. "Not another word," she tells him and gets slowly to her feet. "If you care for me at all you won't talk of this ever again – not to me and certainly not to anyone else." *How could you...I never would have believed...I trusted you.*

It isn't a request, Logan knows, and it tears at him to see the pain he has caused her. "If that's what you want," he nods, watching her leave the conservatory without speaking another word.

Logan has settled himself in the lounge with a book. He is giving Catherine the time and space she needs to assimilate all the information he has given her. And it is there that Catherine finds him less than an hour later.

"Now tell me Charles Llwyd had nothing to do with my mum's murder!" Catherine thrusts a sheet of A4 under Logan's nose, her stance hard and unforgiving.

Logan takes the paper and reads the details on it with utter amazement. "Where on earth did you get this?" He is looking up at Catherine in shocked horror when comprehension dawns. "Oh god, Catherine, tell me you didn't hack into Somerset House?"

"Ok then, I didn't hack into Somerset House." Her face is impassive, her attitude unrelenting. "Look at the birthplace listed for Charles Llwyd – you can't seriously expect me to believe that is a coincidence?" *Not on your fucking life!*

Logan sighs heavily, turning his gaze back to the sheet of paper he still holds. "No, Catherine, I don't. The fact that he was born and raised in Glywyth can't be dismissed as coincidence, but it doesn't alter the fact that he was on the other side of the planet when Harriet Leavesden was murdered."

Catherine turns, walks over to the fireplace and places her hands on the mantelpiece to lean there. "I'm so bloody angry I can't think straight, but there has to be a connection – I just have to find it," she states more to herself than to Logan.

Getting up he moves across the room to stand behind her. Putting gentle hands on her shoulders, he turns Catherine to face him. "I'm sorry that you're angry, and to know that I'm the cause of it, but I promise you, Catherine, hurting you was the last thing I intended."

Her lips tremble as she fights back the tears. "I trusted you and you went behind my back anyway." The heat might have left her voice but it is thick with the hurt that tears at her insides. "Now, I just don't know how I feel." A tear escapes her troubled eyes; Catherine doesn't notice, but Logan does and bends to kiss it away.

Putting his arms around Catherine, he draws her in and is relieved when she doesn't pull away. "I love you so much, I just wanted to give you what I've always had – a parent's love and pride; I never dreamed I'd find a sibling." He hugs her tighter and is delighted to feel her snuggle into him. "Don't shut me out, Catherine," he pleads softly, "I want to help you find the connection to Llwyd."

Catherine notes his referral to 'Llwyd' instead of Charles and the hardening of his tone. "So you do believe me?" she asks with cautious optimism, shutting out all mention of her estranged family.

"I believe there has to be more to this than meets the eye," he confirms, and taking her face between his hands kisses her tenderly.

# Chapter Eight

It has been a week since Catherine contacted Inspector Harper with her new findings and she is growing more and more frustrated. "How can they believe it's not him?" she asks Logan for the hundredth time. "I gave them enough proof to hang the man – he was born in Glywyth, he still had relatives living in the area when the torture assaults on young boys and youths occurred," she raises her eyes and hands to the heavens in a hopeless plea, "and I know it was his voice." *For fucks sake, will someone just listen to me?*

Logan watches as Catherine continues pacing the lounge. "I can't even imagine how you must be feeling," he leans forward in his chair and catches hold of her hand when she makes to stride past him again, "but I do know that we need to get out for a while. We're both going stir crazy, locking ourselves away in my office spending hours on the computers reading about the most horrific and gruesome crimes against humanity." Logan tugs on her hand until she sits on his lap then leans back in the armchair taking Catherine with him.

Enfolded in Logan's strong arms Catherine can almost believe that she really is safe from harm; but that voice is not only haunting her dreams, it haunts her every waking moment. "He's out there," she states softly, "and he's waiting for me."

Later that day, Logan virtually drags Catherine kicking and screaming to buy a new gown for Arthur Kingsley's retirement party.

"I still don't see why I can't wear the one I wore last time. It's practically brand new, I've only worn it once and it cost a bloody fortune," Catherine states emphatically.

"I've already told you," Logan repeats calmly for the umpteenth time, "it isn't the 'done' thing. A lot of the people who were at Robert's party will be at Arthur's and, as lovely as you looked in it, you can't appear in the same gown."

"Don't see why not," Catherine states obstinately, and stands resolutely unmoving outside the boutique that Logan had brought her to previously, "all that etiquette stuff you're talking about, it's just another word for snobbery and stuffed shirts. The people who follow it probably have more money than sense, if you ask me!" *Not that anyone is or I wouldn't bloody be here!*

"Mmm," Logan considers Catherine until she shifts uncomfortably.

"What? What?" she repeats when Logan just continues to study her.

"Mmm," is all he eventually says again and begins moving to circle her.

"Will you stop with the 'mmm' shit," Catherine snaps out, and then begins to turn with him as he attempts to step around her. "What the fuck – Logan you are freaking me out!"

"I have just the dress in mind," he smiles eventually. "I thought about buying it for you the last time we were here; if it's still on the rack we'll call it fate."

With that, Logan opens the shop door and steps inside waiting for Catherine to follow. *Bloody buggering hell!*

"You are not buying me anything," she growls at him under her breath as the same sales assistant walks towards them as served them the last time.

She gives them a welcoming smile, and asks if there is anything in particular that she can help them with. "No..." Catherine begins, but is overruled by Logan's swift interruption and the winning smile he gives to the sales woman.

"Yes, actually – the last time we were in you had a beautiful pewter coloured gown with a cowl neck and very simple lines," he explains, ignoring the deepening frown on Catherine's face, "do you still have it?"

The sales woman's face beams. "I know just the one, and you're lucky, we do still have it." Then she leads the way up the stairs to the first floor.

"Why lucky, aren't there any other idiots out there willing to spend an arm and a leg..." Catherine breaks off and stops in front of a manikin dressed in the pewter evening gown. Her jaw has dropped and when she eventually finds her voice again she says, "You've got to be kidding, right?" But when she looks from Logan to the sales clerk and back again she sees that they aren't.

The sales clerk turns to Logan, and with a nod of approval tells him, "I remember the dress size, I'll just go and get it for you."

"Well, you had me fooled," Catherine sniggers, "a crossdresser, eh? Just remember the rules, you have to show me once you've got it on...then I'll tell you honestly if it suits you."

She is laughing now, and Logan's cheeks pink up despite himself. "For that you get to try on a few others

I've got my eye on," he tells her, and enjoys watching her squirm at the thought. "Now behave yourself or I'll make you try on the whole lot."

"As if," Catherine chokes out as the sales woman comes back, but she looks nervously over at Logan all the same.

"If you'd like to come with me," the sales woman holds out a hand to indicate the changing room, "I've also brought you the correct underwear for the dress."

Catherine's eyes goggle. "The dress has its own underwear...?" *Bloody hell!*

Smiling her understanding, and remembering Catherine's inexperience with clothing of the feminine kind, the sales woman explains. "The underwear is designed not to have a negative impact on the lines of this type of dress. It would be a shame to spoil something so lovely with ugly lines and bulges." As they move towards the dressing room she continues, "I was wondering about the underwear I picked out for you on your previous visit – is it to your liking?"

"It certainly is," Logan chimes in, and receives a back handed slap to his stomach for his trouble. Letting out a groan and a chuckle, he sits down to wait.

When the sales woman emerges, Logan points out a couple of other gowns that he likes the look of and smiles his thanks when she goes off to get them. "Logan..." he hears his name shrieked from the changing rooms, "...are you completely off your fucking rocker? Have you even seen the price tag on this thing?" Catherine asks as she walks towards him wearing the gown.

His expression is one of stunned pride. "Whatever it is...," he stands up gaping at her, "...it's worth every single penny."

She gives him an 'oh yeah' smile, and then blushes when she realises that he means it. "You...you like it?" she asks hesitantly.

His warm brown eyes have melted at the site of her, moving down then up her body taking in every beautiful inch of her. "Like is too mundane a word," he tells her quietly, moving forward slowly. "You are beautiful, and the dress is amazing...but together," he breathes a sigh and shakes his head, "...you look stunning."

The sales woman stands to one side, the other dresses Logan has asked to see draped carefully over her arms. He follows Catherine's eyes as they move to regard the woman, and gives an apologetic smile. "I'm sorry to have put you to the trouble, but we won't be needing those," and turning back to Catherine, touches her cheek tenderly, "this one is absolutely perfect."

They don't notice the sales woman leave or hear her utter, "Quite so," as she makes to return the unwanted gowns.

Joining her at the till after Catherine has changed back into her own clothes, the sales woman looks a little bit uncertain. She has packed the gown and underwear carefully in a box and put it on the counter ready for them, but which one, she asks herself, will be paying for it?

Catherine laughs as she correctly guesses the reason for the sales woman's poorly hidden consternation. "It's ok," she looks at the badge the woman is wearing, "Selma – is it ok for me to call you that?" and Selma nods with a warm smile. "Ok Selma, well, we already struck a bargain," and looking back as Logan approaches Catherine lets out another laugh. "I'm giving Logan here a dose of his own medicine, and in return he gets to pay for my dress."

"His own medicine...?" Selma asks tentatively, looking from one to the other.

Logan steps up with his credit card in hand. "What Catherine means is...,"

"What I mean is...," she interrupts excitedly, "...I, me, moi...," she laughs prodding herself in the chest, "...get to take him shopping for a change, and I can't wait."

Even Selma allows herself a quiet laugh. "I'm sorry, sir," she apologises to Logan as she takes the proffered credit card.

"Not to worry, Selma," and makes the woman stand tall with pride at the use of her name, "Catherine is insisting she be allowed to buy me a new suit for the function we'll be attending in a couple of weeks – when I've already told her that I own a million of the damn things." An exaggeration maybe, he thinks, but not by much.

"Well, now you'll own a million and one," Catherine smiles wickedly as she casts a wink at Selma.

The tailors that Logan prefers is not more than a ten minute walk away, and so they enjoy a bit of window-shopping along the way.

"You would look great in those," Logan points to a manikin in one of the shops. "We have time if you'd like to try them on," he offers.

"They're trousers," Catherine exclaims, then looking at Logan she has to laugh. "Delaying tactics? You must be desperate if you're willing to let me buy trousers."

"Not at all," Logan protests and turns to enter the shop.

However, before he even reaches the door Catherine has hold of his arm and turns him back around. "No way...it's my turn to watch you suffer," she tells him enjoying his obvious reluctance. "You paid for the dress now you pay the piper."

It is obvious to Catherine that Logan is a prized customer. No sooner have they entered the shop than an attendant is at his side. "Mr Sayers," the attendant greets Logan, "how nice to see you again so soon."

"You see," he turns to Catherine, "I told you that I already have new suits."

She looks from him to the box on the seat next to her. "You know...I could always take this back," she tells him, one eyebrow raised in question.

With a resigned sigh, Logan turns back to the male attendant. "It appears I will be needing another suit, Jacob. If you wouldn't mind showing me the sample book?" he asks.

"If you wouldn't mind showing us the sample book," Catherine corrects decisively.

Logan gives Jacob an assenting nod then makes his way over to Catherine. "You are determined to get your pound of flesh," he observes, picking up the box and standing it next to the seat he then sits on.

"Nothing of the sort," she protests innocently. "I just want to help you choose – isn't that what you do for me?" Her eyes twinkle with mischief and the hint of a smile.

Logan doesn't get the chance to answer as Jacob comes back with the sample book and offers it to them. It is large, and when open spreads across both their knees. "I already have one in that," Logan tells Catherine when she looks hopefully at a lovely charcoal coloured fabric.

"Then show me what you haven't got," she frowns over at him.

Logan does so and without much ado, Catherine decides on the one she likes best. "That would be perfect," she enthuses, and is pleased to see that Logan is nodding his approval.

"The depth of the pewter would complement your gown," he muses; then considers the fabric, feeling the quality and imagining its effect when worn next to the much paler pewter of Catherine's gown. "You have quite an eye for colour," he compliments her.

Catherine scoffs loudly. "Well don't sound so surprised, I'm not a complete moron." *Just because I know zilch about fashion and girl clothes.*

Giving the book back to Jacob, having indicated the fabric they have chosen, Logan turns back to Catherine and takes her by surprise. "There is nothing moronic about you," he states before taking her face between his large gentle hands and kissing her firmly on the mouth.

Catherine gives an embarrassed laugh, sure that her cheeks are flaming red. "Logan...we're in a shop," she admonishes giving his thigh a slap for good measure.

She might have swatted a fly on him for all the notice he took. "Mmm, shame that," his lips pucker up and his eyes regard her lustily.

Catherine hastily holds a hand over her mouth and coughs loudly to mask his words and indicate that they are no longer alone. *Flaming Nora!*

"We have that particular fabric in stock, sir," Jacob tells Logan, then turns to include Catherine in the conversation. "Will you be requiring your first fitting today?"

Catherine looks amazed, but Logan is obviously used to such a speedy service. "This afternoon, if you can fit me in, Jacob," Logan confirms. "We're staying in town for a late lunch, how does a couple of hours from now sound?"

"Perfect," Jacob gives a small nod of his head, like a modified bow, and moves off to set the wheels in motion.

Picking up the box with Catherine's gown in it, Logan puts a guiding hand to her back and ushers Catherine out of the shop.

"That is so not fair," she states grumpily. "You didn't even have to do anything. Why didn't that man at least take your measurements?"

"Because he has them already," Logan sighs. "I keep trying to tell you, I already have a number of new suits. You could just pick out the one you want me to wear from them – suits are damnably expensive,"  he warns, not at all happy at the prospect of Catherine footing such a hefty bill.

"About as expensive as designer evening gowns I expect." Catherine gives Logan a look that tells him not to waste his breath.

Logan just smiles mischievously. "I'd try them all on for you in the privacy of our bedroom," he offers with a wink.

Her face tips up to regard him, a frown on her forehead and one eye closed as if giving his offer serious consideration. "Mmm...," she murmurs mimicking him, "...good offer, but no can do. After all the torture you've put me through, buying girl clothes then making me wear the damn things all the time, I deserve some payback." Her smile turns decidedly fiendish. "Does Jacob stick you often when he pins the suit on you?"

They have a light lunch at a nearby hotel. Logan is known here too, Catherine observes on their arrival. The staff are all smiles and ready to do his every bidding. "Doesn't it ever get on your nerves?" she asks over a glass of white wine they are enjoying after the meal. "I mean, don't you find it a bit spooky everyone knowing who you are?" *Gives me the chills and it's not even me their all smiling at.*

Shaking his head, Logan says, "Not at all, but then I don't think I've ever really thought about it." He looks at his watch and grimaces. "We'd better make a move, by the time we walk back Jacob will be ready for us."

"Do they always do the first fitting on the same day?" Catherine asks as they near the tailors. "It seems a bit of a quick turn-around considering they have to cut it out and basically put it together."

Logan looks uncomfortable. "It's a service they offer but at considerable cost, I'm afraid I didn't think of that."

"So," she looks deliberately worried, "does that mean it's going to cost me an arm and two legs instead of just an arm and a leg?" The look of deep concern on Logan's face makes Catherine relent with a chuckle. "Will you stop worrying – I'm only teasing. According to Ben I have enough in the bank to go out and pay cash money for a brand new Mini Metro; which, like you, he keeps encouraging me to do." *Men!*

They reach the tailors shop and Logan still doesn't look happy. "Ok, ok," she laughs, "it wasn't a Metro it was a Mercedes, or some such happy shit."

"We need to talk about your finances," Logan tells her, still looking serious as he holds the door of the shop open for her.

Jacob greets them with his usual dour face. "I have everything set up for you in fitting room number three," he tells Logan. "There is a more comfortable seating area nearby, madam, if you would care for some tea or coffee?" he offers Catherine.

But she is already shaking her head and nods it towards Logan. "I go where he goes." *No way am I missing all the fun.*

Jacob's expression actually shows some signs of life when he turns questioning eyes to Logan. "Sir...?" is all he says.

Back at Logan's house, just a couple of hours later, Catherine still cannot stop smiling. "I find your enjoyment of my discomfort somewhat disturbing," Logan tells her as he lets them both in the front door.

"Don't give me that," she laughs then reaches up to put her arms around his neck. "You just don't like me paying the bill; chipped away at that masculine pride you wear like a suit of armour." *You and every other bloody man!*

Logan ducks his head to plant a silencing kiss on her triumphant lips then gets more than he bargained for.

Catherine is hungry and food is definitely not on the menu, Logan is. She deepens the kiss so forcefully that he rocks on his heels but isn't slow at catching on. His tongue begins to plunder as his hands find her breasts through the cotton dress and before long they are both breathing heavily.

"Bed...?" Logan suggests.

"Race you," Catherine challenges and speeds off laughing.

She is in the bedroom with her dress pulled off over her head when Logan walks in. He laughs at her mischievous grin, "Eager I see," he walks slowly over to Catherine.

"Maybe," she teases, "or perhaps I'm just feeling the heat."

Pretending nonchalance, Logan veers off towards the bathroom. "In that case perhaps I have time to take a shower first?"

Catherine isn't having that. "Not on your life," she laughs then instead of unbuttoning his shirt she grabbed two hands full and tears it open, the buttons flying off everywhere. Her mouth and hands explore his expansive chest with glee. "You'll only need another one after I've finished with you."

He is delighted with the way Catherine has grown in confidence in the bedroom and is happy to oblige her in any way that pleases her. "Be gentle with me," he protests as she drags him over to the bed and pushes him back onto it.

"Not a chance, big boy," she grins pulling his trousers off after discarding his shoes, "you're all mine until I'm finished with you." With that, she releases him then strokes him slowly up and down without taking her eyes from his. She loves to watch his brown eyes soften as they darkened with pleasure, the power she has over him always intoxicating. "I'm going to do whatever I want to you and you will just have to lie there and take it." *Mmm.*

His breathing is already shallow and his heart rate raised, but when she dips her head to take him into her mouth both seem to stop for a mind numbing second. "Catherine you're killing me," he tells her, not sure that he isn't speaking the truth. She is using her teeth, her tongue and her lips one minute then working him hard with her mouth the next.

"Mine," she tells him as she raises herself to straddle him, "all mine." He reaches up to cup her breasts but she bats his hands away. "I'm taking not giving this time so keep your hands to yourself," she orders then takes his mouth with hers and uses her tongue as she's felt him do to her so many times. She is climbing as high as a druggie on heroin and the heat in her loins is reaching fever pitch. Only when she can stand it no more does she give in to her need to feel him inside her.

He groans loudly when the heat of her surrounds him and has to fight not to lose control. "Catherine...," he begs but cannot manage to utter another word. She takes him in slowly, deeply, enjoying the sensation of him filling her, and then just as slowly lifts herself almost releasing him and continues this rhythm until her control breaks.

Pushing down hard Catherine rides him as if her life depends on it; her head flung back as she holds onto his wrists and he holds hers to give her leverage. Their unified cries as their bodies erupt are loud and unrestrained, the fall back to earth slow and wondrous.

It takes several minutes for their minds and bodies to return to any semblance of normalcy. Logan's arms hold her to him and his heart is full to bursting with a love he's felt for no other woman. "Stay with me, Catherine," he whispers into her hair. "Make this your home and live with me in it forever." His large gentle hand continues to stroke her back then moves over her bottom and gives it a squeeze, "I'd be all yours to do with as you will whenever the fancy takes you." He gives a soft chuckle but they both know he is not joking.

Lifting her head up to look at him, Catherine's eyes are troubled. "Can I have some time to think about it? I mean, you don't want a yes or no right now, do you?" she rushes on nervously. *Fuck. I don't know anything about living with a man. How the bloody hell do I know if it's a good idea!*

He is hurt that she needs to think about it, but Logan can see that if he pushes her on it the answer will be a reflexive no. Instead, he smiles and places a kiss on the tip of her nose. "Take as long as you need. I love you, Catherine, and I want you in my life for as long as I can – for all eternity if the god's permit." However, he can see the troubled soul that is Catherine, and knows it isn't going to be as easy as that.

# Chapter Nine

The night of Arthur Kingsley's retirement party comes around all too soon. With Logan now almost permanently at her side, Catherine is growing in confidence, finding herself actually looking forward to the night out. At least it will be a break from the harrowing trawling of the internet. Reading about the kinds of brutal murders that have been committed in the last twenty-five years is gut wrenching work.

Seated in Logan's car, Catherine asks what he has bought Arthur for his retirement. Turning a plain gold, square box, secured with a narrow ribbon in the same colour, over and around in her hands she says, "It doesn't feel like it's got anything in it," then gives it a gentle shake. "Was I supposed to buy him something?" She asks, turning large worried eyes to look accusingly at Logan.

"You didn't say anything about presents." Catherine swivels back around in her seat and huffs loudly. "I suppose this is more of that etiquette, shit. Just something else I should already know about." *Fuck me!*

Logan smiles and reaches over to take her hand, brings it to his lips and kisses each finger in turn. "I've known Arthur for almost all of my thirty-six years," he explains quietly. "He and my father used to be good friends when they were both just starting out; the pair of them struggling to find their own niche in the business world."

"Will your father be there tonight?" Catherine asks, delighted to think she might have an unexpected ally to hand.

However, Logan soon puts a damper on that. "No, no..." he answers quietly "...he hasn't left Lakelands since my mother passed away." *Oh.*

Catherine turns their joined hands over and returns his kisses, one for each of his fingers. "Sorry," she says simply, but does not let go of his hand until they arrive at Arthur's house.

Logan opens the car door for Catherine to step out, taking her hand to help her. When she turns and gets her first full view of the mansion and all the flowers and lights that stylishly bedeck anything that doesn't move, her mouth falls open with a loud cry of " Holy F...OUCH." Jerking away from Logan, she turns on him with rounded, shocked eyes. "You just pinched my ar..." Moving quickly she jerks out of his way as he moves to pinch her again. *And the son-of-a-bitch is actually smiling about it.* "What is with you?" She growls between clenched teeth as she notices a group of people looking their way.

Logan turns one of his brightest smiles on the group, nodding to acknowledge them.  They return his smile readily enough then turn to walk into the entrance hall. "I was just stopping you from saying something you might regret," he says smoothly, turning the full heat of his smile on her now.

"You mean you want me on my best behaviour!" Waggling a long finger under his nose, she narrows her sparkling blue eyes at him. "You're embarrassed by me, admit it," she tells him, but all he does is catch her finger between his teeth to give it a gentle nip before releasing it.

When she makes no move towards entering the house, Logan turns and shakes her shoulders then pulls her into a bear hug. "I could not be more proud of my little fire-cracker," he laughs, then dips to place a kiss on the top of her head. "However, I must admit that I had hoped you might let Catherine come out to play tonight.

Though if you would rather let Colson have her head I have absolutely no objection – just save the fireworks for when I'm around, and don't drink too much alcohol, it doesn't agree with you."

Stunned, she allows herself to be pulled along, muttering that anyone would think she was a petulant schoolgirl instead of a grown woman.

They enter the entrance hall, which has a champagne reception ready to greet them. Before he can stop her, Catherine reaches out to take a crystal flute from the tray of a passing waiter. Logan eyes her cautiously, and then laughs deciding to let the evening play out as it may.

As it happens, Catherine doesn't get the chance to finish even that first drink. Robert Kingsley spots her and whisks her onto the dance-floor before she can object. Logan goes to find Arthur, who he comes across in the orangery, surrounded by well-wishers and thoroughly enjoying all the attention.

"Ah, Logan," Arthur exclaims as he comes into view. "Glad you could make it, my boy. Did you bring that delightful young woman with you? A breath of fresh air, that one," he continues not waiting for Logan to answer. "Doesn't mince her words or put on any airs and graces. You'd never guess she is a millionaire to look at her, would you now?" He laughs heartily, enjoying the insider joke, and gives Logan a playful jab in the ribs with his elbow.

At Logan's incredulous, "Are you sure about that?" Arthur laughs again then says, "Of course I'm sure. She doesn't charge peanuts for the privilege of tapping that incredible brain of hers." He slaps Logan soundly on his back just before his wife dragged him off to 'do the rounds'.

Logan is staggered. Just how much more is there to learn about the wonderful woman that he has so completely lost his heart to? His hesitant smile turns in to a full on grin and hiis already broad chest swells with pride as he acknowledges what he has been too blind to see. Catherine is not just dabbling in the computerised security industry; she and Ben are major players at the top of their game.

So why does she live in the tiniest bedsit he can imagine, and a rented one at that? Moreover, why does she insist on shopping at the Oxfam shop? That revelation had astounded him when she had told him where she got all her baggy jumpers and trousers. Though she hadn't been the least bit embarrassed about it; quite the opposite in fact. She had declared, somewhat vehemently, that she was supporting local charity work and wearing the clothes that she is most comfortable in at the same time. Then she'd asked him if he'd seen the prices the high street shops are charging and declared them to be a 'bloody cheek'.

Logan catches up with Catherine just as everyone is being ushered out to the specially prepared marquee where the sit down meal is being served.

"You look ravishing," he smiles, taking in her silky blonde hair that is starting to get an interesting flick to the longer ends. The heightened colour of her cheeks only serves to make her beautiful blue eyes shimmer more brightly as she laughs up at him breathlessly.

"Thank you kind sir," she curtsies, then kisses him full on the mouth not caring who is watching.

"What was that for?" he asks when she takes a step back from him. "Not that I'm complaining," he informs her, catching her about the waist.

Catherine looks up at him; and even in her high heels, she does still have to look up at him. "I missed you." It comes out as a quiet oath that sounds like she's really saying 'I love you'. *And you taste so damned good.*

The meal is exquisite, and the speeches are mercifully short – except for Arthur's, of course. He has so many people to thank for various generous gifts and for the special friendships that have lasted over many years.

"What did you buy him, you never did say?" She whispers, leaning close to hear Logan's answer. "Season tickets!" she exclaims loudly. "What the bloody hell does he want those for?" she asks, thinking of Logan's rugby team. "I wouldn't have pegged Arthur or his wife as rugby fans. Unless the other one's for Robert," she frowns. "I suppose that might make sense."

Logan laughs and gives her ear a playful tug. "Not that kind of season tickets, you dolt," he tells her fondly. "They are a pair of season tickets to a private box at the Royal Opera House – both Arthur and Miriam love the opera. Perhaps we could go some time – do you like the opera?" Logan asks, then notices that Catherine has stopped listening. Indeed, she has stopped moving at all and her hand, which had been relaxed through his arm a moment before, is now grasping it tightly.

She looks at him then, all the light in her eyes having dimmed behind fearful shadows. "I didn't know he would be here. I'd never have come if I'd known he would be here," she proclaims in a frightened little voice.

"Who are you talking about?" Logan looks around, frantically trying to spot who has put the fear of god in to Catherine. "Catherine, who are you talking about?" He asks again, when she just continues to stare at him.

"Charles Llwyd." It is all she utters before collapsing into Logan's arms.

Catherine awakes to find herself in one of the guest bedrooms of the mansion house. Miriam, Arthur's kindly wife, is looking after her and assuring Logan that she will be all right after a good rest. One of the guests is a doctor and has already checked her over, apparently, but Logan still sounds frantic with worry.

"Logan...?" Her voice is weak but he hears her call out.

"Catherine...?" He has seen her looking drained before but now she looks unearthly. Her normally alabaster skin is now virtually translucent. "You had me worried," he smiles. Once her eyes have focused on him properly he asks, "What was that about Charles Llwyd?" Logan frowns down at Catherine wondering if he heard her right. "Before you fainted...you said something about Llwyd."

"I heard him..." eyes widening with alarm Catherine tries to sit up "...he's here. I heard him," she repeats her voice rising as the memory becomes clearer. *That voice! That voice! That terrible voice!*

Logan is holding her now and he is shaking violently. No. No, she realises, she is the one shaking from head to toe. "Catherine..." Logan is stroking her hair and his voice is soothing "...he was never here. I asked Arthur and Miriam, he was never invited. Arthur does know him but not on a personal basis, apparently...so you couldn't have heard him. It must have been some sort of...of..." He tails off, has no idea what is going on with Catherine. How could he, as a child she witnessed the sort of horrific violence that would cause any stable adult to have a breakdown, the fact that she spent only two and a half years in psychiatric care is to her credit. "Look, you've been having nightmares about this man, maybe that's all this is...some kind of an 'awake' nightmare?" He is clutching at straws and knows it, and so does Catherine.

"So...basically... what you're saying is...I'm crazy as a frigging loony tune!" Her cheeks are now full of colour. Angry colour, Logan notices. "What the fuck do you expect me to do now?" Catherine leaps off the bed, her arms waving wildly in exasperation. "Maybe you should get me locked up again...isn't that what you're really thinking?" Pulling on the ridiculous heels that she has worn to the party, Catherine turns on Logan. "If you don't even believe me how the fuck can you help me?" *Answer me that, Sherlock!*

Turning on her heels with Logan following close behind, Catherine speeds down the staircase. However, on descending the last step Logan spins her around. "Just stop!" Logan is looking pretty angry himself. "I am not saying I don't believe you. I'm just suggesting that there might be an alternative explanation." His brown eyes hold a fiery glint in there dangerous depths, but Catherine is too blinded by her own temper to pay any heed.

Brushing his hand off her arm, Catherine, in a deceptively quiet, almost reasonable voice, bites out, "Let *me* make a suggestion that you would do well to act on. Get the fucking car and take me home!"

Not a word passes between them until Catherine realises that Logan is taking her back to his house. "I asked you to take me home," she states, her temper not having cooled despite the time spent travelling back.

Giving her a sidelong glare, Logan's temper fires up to match Catherine's. "Fine!" He swings the Mercedes round the next roundabout and heads back the way they just came. Five minutes later, they pull up in front of the five-bedroomed house where Catherine rents one of them. He doesn't stop the engine or make any move towards her, and that is just fine with Catherine.

Removing her seat belt with hands that are now trembling with temper, Catherine opens the car door and slides out. Before slamming it shut, she glares back, "Fuck it!" Even before she can turn away, the sleek black Mercedes is disappearing into the night. *Shit!*

Feeling a fool, standing on the pavement in the early hours of the morning in an evening dress, Catherine wheels round then clutches at her heart in fright.

"Ben...what the fuck are you doing here?" Willing her heart to stop trying to claw its way out of her chest, Catherine reaches into her tiny evening bag for her keys. Looking at them reminds her that her damn car is still parked on Logan's drive. Perhaps she can get Ben to drop her round there some time tomorrow when Logan might be at work. It isn't cowardly doing it that way, Catherine reasons to herself, she just can't be arsed to have another run in with him. She has, after all, more important things to do with her time.

Ben sits quietly in the only chair, wicker with a cushion that doesn't quite fit, that Catherine has in her one room all-inclusive living area. He watches her now, pottering about making coffee on her pathetic electric hob. Beneath it is a tiny oven, and to the side is a two-foot square work surface that has to be used for everything. Next to that is the smallest stainless steel sink and single drainer he has ever seen and he can't stem a chuckle.

"Why do you live like this?" he asks as Catherine brings him a steaming cup of black coffee. "You could live in luxury..."

"But I choose to live here," she interrupts, moving to the single bed to sit on it. She looks around. "I have my own bathroom..." she waves a hand towards a shower cubicle fitted into the opposite corner of the room, "...a kitchen, a bed..." she pats the blanket she is sitting on "...the only thing I can't do in here is take a leak," she grins ruefully. "You take money far too seriously," she tells Ben, and gets herself more comfortable, leaning back against the wall.

"And you don't take it seriously enough," he scolds, then smiles. "Not that you ever have. I couldn't believe the pittance you were charging when we first met – your clients were ripping you off instead of the other way round."

"I'm not in this for the money. It just happens to be a handy by-product of something I actually enjoy doing."

Catherine is being completely sincere. She never had much growing up alone with her mum, after she'd been murdered Catherine had had even less. The psychiatric unit had all kinds of everything she could ever have wanted, except for her mother. And she'd had to come to terms with the fact that there was no going back – no one was going to come up to her shouting 'hey kid, fooled yah!' Not that anyone had ever come. She had gotten used to spending a lot of time looking out of her bedroom window.

Foster care had not been much better. You had to be able to move from one house to another at the drop of a hat, so it wasn't a good idea to have lots of possessions. More often than not everything she'd had fitted into a couple of Tesco carrier bags. Her most important needs were more skills really. Like, how not to intrude into the resident family that was offering her a so called home.

They didn't really want her there but the benefits they claimed made it worth the hassle, she supposed. However, the one thing you had to learn was, never back down. Once you did, you were fodder for every bully who wanted to take their own frustrations, tempers or loneliness out on someone else with their fists. That had been a lesson she'd learned fast and still lived by.

Ben watches the emotions playing over her face. He has loved Catherine from the first time he laid eyes on her; but he soon learned that if he made a move on her he would be out the door and his feet wouldn't touch the ground. Catherine had been running scared. Ben had sussed that right off. It has taken him a lot longer to piece her past together from the little tit-bits she lets drop in an unguarded moment – but they are rare. "What is it, Colson...you look haunted?" *As usual.*

"Colson...?" Ben repeats when she gives no reply.

Instead of answering his question, Catherine asks him one of her own. "You never did tell me why you were waiting outside the house for me? Did you lock yourself out or something equally daft?" She knows he hasn't but doesn't want her question to sound like a pervy accusation.

"No." he states looking suddenly uncomfortable. "I took a chance that you might be home, that's all. You haven't been into the office since...well, since we had that god awful row."

"I'm actually really glad to see you." A smile steals across his face and Catherine continues quickly. "I mean, I could use your help." He doesn't interrupt and she ploughs on in case her courage fails. "First, I need to fill you in on a few very personal things."

Ben leans forward in the chair. "I think I may already know some of it," he interrupts then sits back as Catherine looks at him, obviously annoyed.

"Just give me a minute, Ben. If I'm going to do this I need you to let me tell you in my own way." Ben nods his assent and Catherine steels herself against the pain she knows the re-telling will bring. "You already know I have no family," she begins steadily. "I think you may already know, too, that I was in foster care from the age of twelve until I was seventeen, and that's when I moved here." Her hands sweep the room again. "This was, is, my first home."

"I had heard most of that," Ben confesses. "And I had sort of heard that your mother had died. But that's about it really."

"My mother was murdered," she clarifies, "and I was in the room when it happened."

Ben gasps loudly, realising the significance immediately. "You were left alive by the murderer and stayed with her while she died?"

The smile she gives him is ugly and sneering. "You could say that...or you could say that a performance was given especially for me." Catherine can see that Ben is full of questions but holds a hand up to stop him voicing them. "Just let me tell it my own way," she reiterates then begins again.

"I was home alone when the man broke in. He didn't seem to know I was there, at first. My mum was working just down the road, and I prayed she would come back soon." That prayer has haunted Catherine for years. She has blamed herself for wanting so desperately for her mum to come home and make whoever was in the house go away. Has believed she somehow wished it all on her.

"Anyway," she shakes off the unpleasant thought, "she did come home, and she did confront the man. But he just laughed, grabbed her and brought her into the bedroom where I was hiding under the bed. After taping her hands and feet to the bed and putting more tape over her mouth, he raped her." She hears Ben's muffled, "Oh my god," but ignores it.

She doesn't tell him how the bastard hurt her mum so badly that she screamed the whole time, or that instead of climbing out from under the bed to help her she'd curled herself up in a ball, closed her eyes tight and put her hands over her ears.

"I don't know if he knew I was there the whole time, but as soon as it was over he reached under the bed and pulled me out by my feet." Catherine furrows her brow, trying to recall that part of the memory. "I can't remember ever making a sound, he just seemed to know I was there; and that's when the nightmare began." She takes a deep, steadying breath before carrying on. "I don't know where he got the tape – brought it with him I suppose – but he used a lot of it to tie me to a chair. He forced my legs open, commented on how lovely my white cotton knickers were, then taped each leg separately to the outside of the front legs of the chair. I was so exposed, so terrified of what I thought he might do to me." Her sudden, self-deprecating laughter made Ben jump. "Sorry, I just can't get over it even now – I was so busy worrying about me that it never occurred to me that my mum was still in danger; never occurred to me that the son-of-a-bitch might actually kill her."

Shaking her head in wonder at her own selfishness, Catherine takes a second or two to swallow a huge ball of shame before she can continue.

However, Ben beats her to it. "Are you crazy?" Ben is on his feet now, not attempting to go over to her or offer comfort, he knows she won't tolerate that. But he will be damned if he'll let her carry the blame for what some monster did or for any thoughts of self-preservation she might have had. "Are you totally nuts?" Catherine winces at that but realises Ben is unaware of her time in psychiatric care and isn't about to clue him in. Pacing angrily up and down the small room he finally comes to a stop at the foot of her bed. "Just how old were you when this happened?"

"Ten," she replies, "or near as damn it."

"Ten," he repeats incredulous. "And you're seriously telling me that you think a ten year old girl could have done anything to stop that maniac from doing exactly what the hell he pleased? He'd have snapped your pretty young neck in a heartbeat, by the sound of him!" he grinds out, angry on Catherine's behalf.

Catherine appreciates his anger. No one has ever gotten angry on her account before; well, except Logan, she has to admit if only to herself. "Do you want to hear the rest or do you need to rant some more?" she asks quietly.

Ben shakes his head and retakes his seat saying a very quiet, "Sorry, won't happen again."

"Ok, well, I'm not going to go into too much detail about the rest of it...I just can't right now. Suffice to say, after taping my legs open to the chair I was sitting on, he forced my arms around each side of the high back and taped my hands together real tight."

Catherine remembers the pain and unconsciously rubs at them. "He tore off another piece of tape and fastened it across my mouth...though I don't know how he got it to stick, the tears had been flowing the whole time and never stopped. Then he pulled my mum up by the hair, her eyes were closed, I wasn't sure if she was pretending or if she really was asleep – I didn't realise till much later that he'd knocked her out cold."

Another gasp from Ben gives her pause, but Catherine is determined to get it all out. "He dropped my mum back on the bed then actually left the room. I was amazed. Was that it? Was he really gone?"

She looks across at Ben then. "That's when you could have called me crazy," she tells him with a knowing shake of her head. "I actually believed the son-of-a-bitch had gone, but he'd only gone as far as the outer hallway to get his tool bag. Then he brought my mum's small coffee table in and set his terrible instruments out in precise rows right in front of me."

Ben's hand flies to cover his mouth, his grey eyes growing wet with tears that he is fighting valiantly.

"My mum was still out of it, and by the way he looked at me I knew they were meant to hurt me. I had never been so terrified in all my young life. I think he enjoyed that.  He'd pick them up in turn, opening blades and cutting a piece of paper to prove how sharp they were. Or he'd open and close various types of pliers and cutters – I know now that some of them were the type of cutters you would use for pruning roses, or some such happy shit. Anyhow, he waved them right under my nose and told me, in detail, exactly what he was going to do with each tool, then moved over to my mum's bed and began cutting her toes off one by one."

She has to stop. Her chest is so tight she can barely open her lungs enough to take another breath. But she does, and the next and the next. She can't look at Ben now; knows she can't hold it together much longer and seeing his shock and horror will only heighten her own.

"As I said, he put plenty of masking tape over her mouth before he raped her, and taped each wrist and ankle to the four corners of the bed. She couldn't move and she couldn't scream; at least not loud enough to make anyone else but me and that monster hear."

She does look up at Ben then, too lost in the horror of her tale to see his freely flowing tears. "I don't know that it could have been any worse to hear those screams right out loud; her eyes told me everything I didn't want to know. She didn't have any knickers on; he'd ripped those off during the rape, and I thought he might rape her again." Catherine's head is already shaking when she says, "He didn't, but what he did with those tools of his was much worse." Her mind gradually returns from the hell she's had to relive in the telling of her mother's suffering, enough to focus on why she is telling Ben in the first place.

"I don't know where Logan and I stand with each other as of tonight," she explains, "but we've been doing a lot of computer digging in an attempt to track that fucking monster down. But..." Catherine lifts both her hands palms up in the air then lets them fall into her lap in a helpless gesture.

Ben draws a tissue out of his pocket, wipes his eyes and cheeks then uses what is left to blow his nose. He cannot believe it, he looks at Catherine and her eyes are dry. Her shoulders and back are uncharacteristically slumped, but other than that, she is keeping herself together a lot better than he is.

"I always knew there was something deep and dark and seriously disturbing in your past, but, I never dreamed...I never put your surname together with that terrible murder." He states, somewhat bemused. "I can remember my mother was terrified of her own shadow after that. In fact, all my mates' mums were the same, come to think of it." His head is shaking at his own stupidity. "I should have put it together; I'm sorry I didn't."

"That doesn't matter. What I need to know is, will you help me to find him? Can you help me, without hurting yourself in the process?" She is desperate and yes, she has to admit, selfish enough to take advantage of Ben's first-class tech' skills if he is willing to offer them.

"I'd do anything for you," he tells her honestly. "There's no point beating about the bush, I've already told you that I'm in love with you, if all I'm allowed to give you is my time then it's yours...as much as you want of it, and more if you ever change your mind about us." He had to keep that option out there. Although, in his heart, Ben already knows that she just doesn't see him that way. He, of course, will never see her any other way.

"Let's keep the status quo the way it's always been," she pleads softly. "You're the best friend I've ever had and I don't want to lose that. If we can manage to ride this out there's no reason we can't carry on the business and become even more successful. I know you put the idea of taking on more staff forward months ago, and I'm going to give it some serious consideration; even more so as I won't be back in the office until this is over." She didn't realise she was going to say that; but now that she has it seems like the best way to go. "In fact, just do it Ben. Hire whomever you think is best. You always have held the financial reins of the business, why stop now?" She is actually smiling now, a new positive surge coursing through her veins. "Use my office; it'll fit two at a pinch, if you think that's what we need."

Ben smiles too. "We're going to need bigger premises," he observes with an ambitious glint in his grey eyes, "pity we didn't think of it sooner." When he sees Catherine wince, he changes the subject quickly. "I bet you don't even know how much is in your own bank account?" he teases, lightening the mood.

"Do too," she responds rashly, then plucks a figure out of the air that she thinks might be somewhere in the ballpark. "Must be nearing my first million by now," she jokes, "unless you're not as good at the finances as you're always telling me you are?"

"Not even close," he scoffs at her pathetic guess. "And I'm even better than I let on – try 14.5 million," he states with no little satisfaction when her mouth gapes open. "Better close your mouth I saw a fly in here earlier."

Catherine laughs, then hesitates, then laughs again. "You're not kidding," she says stating the obvious. "Just how much do we charge for our services – it has to be exorbitant whatever it is?" *Well fuck me, who'd have thought!*

"One day, when you're really interested, I'll take you through it all in detail. Until then, let's get back to the business at hand. Why now?" he asks. "Your mother's been gone for something like fifteen years, what's caused you to start looking for him now?"

She tells him about the man she heard talking with Logan at Lakelands, about his distinctive voice and how it had shaken her to the core when she'd recognised it.

"Ok, so Logan told you who he is and did a lot of digging into his background and whereabouts at the time of your mother's murder; and he was out of the country, you say?"

"I don't say," Catherine corrects, "I didn't do the digging – but I do trust Logan in this. I don't believe he would have told me that unless he was one hundred percent positive." *But then I didn't believe he'd ever go behind my back to find my dad, and a sister I never knew I had. This love crap stinks!*

"And tonight...?" Ben asks.

Catherine eyes him, trying to decide if he is prying for personal reasons or genuinely trying to help. She decides on the latter and tells him what had transpired at Arthur Kingsley's retirement party.

"So, you don't think Logan believed you when you told him you'd heard that same voice in close proximity to where you and he were sat," Ben summarises, the inflection in his voice casting Logan in a very poor light.

"I suppose you could say that," Catherine admits reluctantly, then unexpectedly comes to Logan's defence. "I wasn't exactly behaving rationally at the time. He probably had good cause to think I was having some sort of auditory hallucination. In fact, he told me I'd got my 'Colson' head on as opposed to my 'Catherine' head," she smiles nervously. "He has this theory that when I'm in a mood or misbehaving, as he calls it, that's when I have my Colson head on. Conversely, my Catherine persona is supposed to be all sweetness and light and only mildly argumentative." She gives a loud snort then stops short when Ben actually agrees.

"I'm sorry, my lovely, but he's got you down to a tee," he admits grudgingly. "Now, where do we go from here? Can we get a copy of the guest list by legitimate means? Or do we need to do a bit of 'off record' digging? I'd go off record," Ben advises, "you never know who old man Kingsley, or his son if he hears you've been asking about it might, even innocently, divulge that information to. Why take a chance on it being the one person we wouldn't want to know?"

Catherine gives an almighty yawn that sounds a crack in her jaw. "I'm sorry, Ben, hold on to that thought and any others you have for finding out more information." She yawns again and her sore eyes begin to water. "I need to lie down before I fall flat on my face. I can't remember ever feeling this tired." *Not even after an athletic sex session with Logan. No, stop that. Don't even go there!*

"You're expending a lot of nervous energy would be my best guess," he says as he walks to the door. "Will you be coming into the office tomorrow – I don't mean to work, but we will need to discuss this a lot more?"

Catherine turns her face up to the ceiling. "Damn! Damn! Damn! Damn! Damn! I forgot to mention, my car's still parked on Logan's drive, any chance of a lift in the morning so that I can pick it up?" She cringes as she asks knowing Logan's house will be the last place Ben would want to go. *Fuck!*

But Ben doesn't blink, and that makes Catherine wary. "Not a problem. I'll pick you up at nine; it's already quarter to two and you just said you're out on your feet," he reminds her. "As you are the boss a bit of tardiness in a good cause shouldn't be a problem." He leans in and lays a kiss on her cheek before leaving. Not something he has ever done before, and it leaves Catherine wondering whether Ben isn't taking too much hope from the fact that she and Logan are having a few problems.

She will just have to worry about that tomorrow, and yawns again. Pulling her evening dress off over her head, she lets it puddle on the floor at the side of her bed then climbs gratefully into it. A few seconds after her head touches the pillow Catherine falls into an exhausted sleep, too tired even to dream.

## <u>Chapter Ten</u>

Ben drives none too slowly Catherine notes, pulling her seatbelt even tighter, over to Logan's house. "We're not in any hurry here," she comments after Ben takes a bend at close to fifty mph, "arriving in one piece would be preferable to not arriving at all." *Bloody hell!*

Ben laughs heartily. "I'd never have guessed you'd be a nervous passenger. I've seen you drive, Catherine, and you don't exactly drive like a granny yourself."

"True," she confesses easily, "but then my hands are on the wheel; I wouldn't let me crash and burn!"

He laughs again, and Catherine eyes him speculatively. She can't remember seeing Ben so...so...what, she asks herself. She just can't put her finger on what is worrying her, except that, for a man who is in the company of the woman who has recently rejected him, he is taking it a bit too well.

"Ok, we're here." Ben pulls his sports car in to Logan's drive. It is long and the grounds expansive and Catherine's car is nowhere to be seen. "So, where did you stow it?" Ben asks, and again Catherine finds herself frowning at his chipper tone.

"It was right there." She points to a spot closer to the house. "Now I suppose I'll have to knock on his fucking door to ask him." In a matter of seconds, she has gone from unease to in your face angry. Catherine stomps down the drive, Ben bouncing along behind her, and then raises a fist to bash on the large oak door.

"Now, now," Ben cautions, "let's do this with a little dignity. You don't want him to think he's got the better of you."

Whether he meant to or not, Ben's comment stirs Catherine up even more. She is about to give the door another hammering when it opens, her fist almost smashing into Logan's face.

If only, Ben smiles wickedly, delighted to see Logan's deepening frown when he looks over Catherine's head at him. "Morning Logan, we've just come to collect Colson's car, and on such a lovely day," he adds brightly.

Before Logan can reply with anything more that a snarl, Catherine whirls on Ben. "Fuck it, Ben, I can speak for myself!" then spins back to Logan as he finally speaks.

"Your car is in the left hand side of the double garage," he informs her, having put it there himself the night before. He knew she would have to come to pick it up and had hoped to use that time to talk more reasonably to her. More than that, he'd hoped to get their relationship back on track. It had been lonely in his large bed, which had seemed enormous and so empty without her in it. "I'll take you over," he closes the heavy door behind him and makes to step off the flagstone set in front of it. However, Ben, who has moved imperceptivity forwards, is now standing in his way with his hand held out for the keys Logan is holding.

"I think we can manage." Ben's smile is still in place but markedly slips when Logan virtually walks through him as if he were not there.

"I don't think so," he states on a low growl, and Logan strides off with Ben doing multiple running steps to keep up.

Catherine stands, hands on hips, gaping after the two strutting bull headed men. It is the first time she has seen them side by side. Her head tilts to the right as she considers each in turn. Ben is no short-arse; at six feet, he is considered acceptably tall and his frame is more than acceptably filled out with good toned muscle. But next to Logan, who stands at six feet four and appears to tower over Ben, he looks almost wimpy. Logan has the build of a prop-forward and indeed, Catherine has watched him play in that capacity more than once now.

She can't help the lustful sigh or the flutter in her belly or the heat that is gathering between her thighs; Ben doesn't stand a chance. Focusing on Logan, Catherine watches his long legs eat up the distance to the garages. Even dressed in formal suit trousers and shirt she can clearly see his thigh muscles stretch and flex, his tight buttocks filling those trousers just so. She has a sudden vision, of her hands clenching over them as Logan pounds frantically into her, that almost causes Catherine's knees to buckle.

"Get a grip, girl," she scolds herself, then eyes Logan's wicked arse and wishes longingly that she could.

By the time Catherine catches up with the two men, who are now obviously squaring off, the garage door is open and her old car, clearly visible, is still inside.

"If you two have finished pissing testosterone all over my car," she glares from one to the other of the furious men, "I'll just take my keys," which she does, snatching the dangling bunch out of Logan's hand, "and get out of here."

Opening the driver's door, Catherine makes to get inside, but Logan grasps her arm, none too gently, forcing her to look at him. "Will I see you tonight?" It was a question, but she hears the plea behind it and sees it in his eyes.

It must be mortifying for him to show such weakness in front of a man he considers a rival, she realises and nods before pulling away to get into her car. Firing it up, she puts it into reverse and leaves it to both men to jump out of the way.

"Damn it," Ben exclaims, picking himself up off the floor.

Logan merely smirks with satisfaction and strides back to the house without a backward glance.

For almost the whole of that day, Ben and Catherine plan how they might find her mother's murderer. "Ben, do you really think we can do this?" *Wouldn't the police have found him by now if it were possible? But we did find Harriet Leavesden, and we made the connection. But what now?*

Rounding the desk to put an ostensibly comforting arm across her shoulders, Ben nods firmly. "Try not to worry," he gives her shoulders a squeeze. "I'm going to put some time in on this tonight. We'll get the bastard," he declares adamantly, and enjoys the grateful smile she gives him.

"Thanks Ben, I should have known you'd never let me down," then grimaces when he drops a kiss on her cheek and says, "Never!"

Driving over to Logan's house gives Catherine time to think. She had been angry with him because he hadn't believed her, yet she knows he supports her wholeheartedly. And he loves her; she concedes melting into her seat.

After parking her car on his drive, Catherine is pleased to see Logan waiting for her. The open door casts a warm glow over him and her heart skips a couple of beats. *Jesus, I've missed him so much and it's only been one night and one day. But he's mine, damn it, and I'm his – that's just the way it is!*

There are no recriminating words between them. Just a look is all it takes and the hunger that burns in one calls to the other.

Logan sweeps Catherine up in his arms, carries her up the wide staircase to his bedroom and kisses her so thoroughly that all sanity is lost.

There is only Logan now, and her greedy need for him. There is no fumbling over buttons or clasps, their hands move with surety and with purpose to reveal quickly what they crave.

Gloriously naked, muscles rippling with need, Logan stands diamond hard before her. Catherine drops to her knees, pleasuring Logan until he cries out with the effort of holding himself back, then finds herself lying flat across his bed with those incredibly molten brown eyes devouring every trembling inch of her. "Mine!" he roars in a primal declaration that should have irked. But Catherine reaches up to touch his heart. "Mine!" She echoes, just as possessively.

Then it is Catherine's turn to cry out. The heat between her thighs is now burning out of control. Her head thrashes side to side, her fingers clutching at the sheets, as his mouth finds her centre and plunders it mercilessly.

"Please..." she gasps "...I need you inside me." But his deft fingers replace his tongue and drive her over the first cliff of release.

"You'll never leave my bed again!" It is a demand, and one she willing gives in to.

"Never," she manages to get out. Then his lips crush hers with a depth of passion that effectively seals their pact.

Then he is plunging inside her, ripping screams from her lips that she hears only as dim sounds that someone else is making. She meets his rhythm, beat for lustful beat until, slick with the enormous effort of their passion, they both erupt as one. Home. Safe. Loved.

It is a long time later until either of them moves. Thankfully, Logan has slumped his considerable weight at the side of her, Catherine realises as she traces her fingers across his rising and falling chest, thinking him asleep.

"If you keep doing that we are going to go for a second round." His voice might be lazy, but she can see he is making no idle threat.

She draws her hand down over the bulging sheet and snickers playfully. "I'm up for it, and I can see you certainly are."

Logan hesitates, looking at her for a long contemplative moment. "What did I ever do to deserve you?" he asks, his hand stroking her silky hair that is now long enough for him to run his fingers through.

"Don't say that." Her fingers stop their teasing dance, "Let's just take what we have while we have it, and hold no regrets when it's gone."

Logan props his weight on one elbow to look down on her. She doesn't look upset, has just stated what she sees as the facts. They are happy enough now but she doesn't see it lasting – is he being a complete idiot to think that it can? "I love you, Catherine. That isn't just a phrase I use to please you, it's how I feel."

Realising that she has inadvertently hurt him, Catherine tries to explain. "I just meant that you love me now, but who knows how you'll feel in a year or maybe five years' time?" He is frowning and she can see that she isn't making things any better. "What if you meet someone who's everything I'm not? Someone who knows all about that etiquette stuff who doesn't get mad rather than get hurt." Turning her back to Logan, she pulls the sheet tight around her. "Maybe you love Catherine, but I've been Colson for a long time now – I don't think I know how to change." *I can't be what you want. I only wish I could.*

Logan is dumbfounded. How can she think he would even look at another woman? Putting a gentle hand on her shoulder he tries to roll her back towards him, but Catherine holds herself firm. "I don't know what I've ever done or said that could make you think I would, or could, give any other woman what I've already given to you, but you are so wrong." Logan tries to roll her back towards him again and this time she complies. "I love you more than life, more than I can possibly tell you." His hands move to cup her face, his thumb gently caressing her cheek. "My soul is bound to yours now, I honestly believe that, and I couldn't be happier about it."

Turning fully into his arms, Catherine winds her arms about his neck and holds on for dear life. "I love you so much it hurts, and it scares me," she admits. "If anyone can drive love away it's me, and then where will I be?" *Hurt and alone. Again. Like always.*

Logan manages a small laugh and tightens his arms around her. "I'm going to enjoy proving to you just how much I love you," he smiles into her hair. "Not that I'll let you have everything your own way," he warns with a chuckle, "that would make life boring, and you are never that, my darling Catherine."

Next morning, Catherine is up early and in the shower. She is mulling over the last couple of days, the voice at Arthur's party and Logan's declaration of eternal love. She smiles at the thought of an eternity with Logan, "What a man," she tells the empty room, "and Christ, what a body." Catherine laughs as 'the body' walks in to the wet-room.

"Well you're in a chipper mood," he smiles broadly, as he walks towards Catherine. "Mind if I join you?" He laughs as Catherine crooks a finger at him. "I'll take that as a no."

Logan moves to get some shower gel, but Catherine has beaten him to it. "I already had my wash, this is for you," and she rubs the gel between her hands then begins the task of washing Logan. They are standing face to face and her hands are moving over his broad chest and shoulders in firm circular motions. "Just look at all these lovely muscles," she moves her hands over his biceps and give them a squeeze, "hard as rock." Her hands become busy again, working their way over his abdomen. "And just look at this six pack," Logan lets out a moan as her hands skirt lower but completely ignore his enormous erection. Putting more gel on her hands, Catherine moves them over his sculptured thighs then moves around him to stroke them lovingly over his taught buttocks. Remembering her thoughts of biting his peachy arse when he'd been striding away with Ben at his heels, Catherine decides to act on it and nips him on both cheeks.

Logan leans his hands against the wet-room wall and lets out a huge groan when her hands move under him to cup his balls. "Catherine..." He is struggling to maintain control as she continues her exploration of every part of his body but the one that craves her attention.

Loving the power she holds over him, Catherine eventually relents. Moving to stand in front of Logan, the kiss she gives him is as torturous as her touch. So deep and suggestive, her tongue, teeth and lips drive him wild. "Now," she groans into his mouth, and Logan doesn't need to hear any more.

Hitching her up against the wet-room wall, he plunges into her like a man possessed. There is no finesse, and Catherine doesn't want any. "Harder...," she groans, her hands fasten on his shoulders and her brilliant blue eyes urge him on. Her legs tighten around him as her body begins the climb of ecstasy.

"Now, Catherine...now!"

The wet-room echoes their joint cries of release, no mere sighs of pleasure but guttural screams that reflect the powerful joining of their bodies. As the waves continue to course through them, they sink together in a tangle of arms and legs to the floor.

Neither speaks as the shower continues to rain down on them; both dragging in oxygen like marathon runners at the end of a race.

Catherine surfaces first. "Logan...?" He gives an answering, "Mmm," the dreamy response drawing a satisfied smile from her. "Did you ever experience anything like that before?" she asks shyly, then adds, "With anyone else, I mean?"

When his brown eyes open to regard her, they are dark with residual passion. "Hand on heart," and moves to place it there, "I have never experienced the power of lovemaking that I have with you – but then, I've never loved anyone the way I love you." *Can a woman ask for any more than that?*

They share a tender kiss then Catherine breaks away laughing. "If we don't move our arses will look like prunes – just look at my fingers," she shows him to prove her point.

He kisses them then moves to pull her up with him. "I'm going to have a freshen-up and you can keep your hands to yourself, you pervert," he tells her with mock severity.

It makes Catherine laugh as she moves across to the basin and begins doing her teeth. Looking up into the mirror after rinsing her mouth, Catherine studies her reflection. She looks different somehow.

"Are you looking for wrinkles?" Logan teases, coming up behind her to look in the mirror. "You won't find any; I've banished all your frown lines away and replaced them with smiles," and kisses the top of her head.

"That's it," she tells their reflection, "I was trying to figure out what is different about me, and it's that easy," she turns and put her arms around his waist, "I'm happy."

That simple statement tears at him. He hates that she has suffered so much when his own life has been so easy in comparison. Logan enfolds her in his strong arms and makes a silent pledge to make his Catherine smile at least once every day. "And so am I," he tells her.

By the time they have dressed and talked about their plans for the day, it is getting on for eight o'clock.

Catherine sniffs the air. "I smell bacon and eggs," she tells Logan before heading out of the bedroom door.

"That'll be Mrs Baines; she'll be here for most of the day today." He follows Catherine down the stairs and out into the conservatory having said good morning to his housekeeper along the way. "When are you planning to call Inspector Harper?" he asks Catherine as she pours him a cup of filter coffee.

"I'm not sure," she replies while pouring a cup for herself. "I need to check my emails. Ben said he'd send anything he found in an email and I'm hoping it will include Arthur's guest list."

Logan frowns, not just at the mention of Ben, but also at the suggestion that he might have gotten hold of a copy of the guest list. "When did he go to see Arthur – or his secretary?"

"Err...I don't think he was planning to ask them for it...exactly," she says quickly, then stuffs another fork full of eggs and bacon into her mouth so that she won't be able to answer any more questions for a while. Logan does not say a word and eventually she does have to swallow. "This is really good; you should eat yours before it goes cold."

"Catherine...?" is all he says, but it's enough to make her squirm. *Shit!*

"Well it's not like he's going to get caught," she defends Ben's decision to hack into Arthur's secretary's computer. "Ben's as careful as I am, and it's not like he did it for fun," she states waving her fork at Logan. "He took a risk for me, to help me catch that butchering bastard!"

He'd bet Ben was clamouring to offer his services, and making himself out to be a big hero, Logan thinks sarcastically, but is wise enough to keep his thoughts to himself. "So, are you planning to hand the list over to the Inspector? You'll hardly be able to tell him from where you obtained it."

She can tell he is really pissed. His 'Etonian' voice becoming more pronounced when he is. "I'm hardly likely to do anything as dumb as that, but yes, I'll make sure he gets a copy of it." Shovelling in the last mouthful, Catherine jumps up taking her coffee with her. "You finish off, I just wanna get my laptop," she mumbles through her breakfast, and then she is gone.

Logan sits, pushing his food around his plate until Mrs Baines asks him if he is finished. "Sorry, not much of an appetite," he explains lamely.

"Not coming down with something, I hope?" Mrs Baines is a motherly sort, and as Logan doesn't have one of his own, she finds herself stepping in now and then.

"Just a touch of Benitis," he huffs sitting back in his seat, "but I'll take care of it."

"I bet you will," she tells Logan, surprising him when she laughs. "With my Larry it was Carlitis, a young man I met at uni'," and laughs again when Logan's eyebrows shoot up. "Yes, I went to university," she tells him proudly, "I wasn't always an old widow-woman."

"What did you study?" he asks, forgetting his own troubles for a while.

"Well, I started off doing art and design," she smiles broadly, "it was all the rage in the sixties."

"Ahh," Logan chuckles teasingly, "you were a flower child."

"For a while I was," she admits while clearing the pots, "and then life took a more serious turn and I decided to change my degree to Psychology and worked with very young troubled children for many happy years."

"So, how did Larry take care of his Carlitis?" Logan asks intrigued.

Mrs Baines actually blushes and turns in to the kitchen, ostensibly to put the pots next to the sink, but taking the time to compose herself as well. "My Larry was a jealous man," she explains, "and not at all given to violence," she defends her late husband. "He just came across Carl and me talking on campus one afternoon, and lost it – punched his lights out right then and there," and she demonstrates with a fist smacking loudly into her open palm.

Logan is laughing heartily, amazed that this lovely woman has worked for him for the last five years and he'd had no idea about her. "So what happened after – did you and Larry walk off into the sunset, as it were?"

"We did not!" she bristles, her face a picture of disdain. "I gave Larry a piece of my mind and tended to Carl as best I could. Poor lad had a broken nose on account of me and Larry should have known better."

"But, I thought...?" Logan frowns in confusion, trying to fathom out what he missed.

Mrs Baines gives him an indulgent smile. "Well of course I looked after Carl, but there was never anyone but

Larry for me." She chuckles mischievously then says, "I let him stew for a while, just to let him know I didn't hold with violence, and then I let him sweet-talk me into going out with him again." A blush steals in to her cheeks again as she says, "Truth be known, I was quite flattered to think Larry would do such a thing over me, but then he always was a romantic soul." Her face has become winsome with remembering.

Logan watches as Mrs Baines returns to the kitchen, her thoughts miles away with 'her Larry'. He has just stepped into the hallway when he hears his name called from the lounge.

"There you are," Catherine says as he enters the room, "I just ran up to your office looking for you – surely you haven't been eating breakfast all this time?" Then Catherine remembers why she has been looking for him. "Bloody hell, sorry Inspector, Logan's here now so we can carry on." Glad that it isn't a video phone, she rolls her eyes and sits down.

"Ah, right you are then," Inspector Harper's voice comes out of the phone's speaker, "good-morning to you Mr Sayers."

"Good-morning to you too, Inspector," Logan
replies in kind, "but just Logan will do fine."

Catherine interjects the stiff formalities grating on her. "Ok, let's get down to it," she demands briskly, "you've had a chance to look at the list from the party, are there any names on it that match with your own enquiries?" Logan perches himself on the arm of her chair, and Catherine takes his hand with both of hers and holds on tight with fearful anticipation.

"As a matter of fact, there is a name of interest," Inspector Harper confirms, but does not seem inclined to enlighten them further.

Catherine squeezes Logan's hand even tighter, her nerves jangling waiting for the Inspector to tell them who it is. When he doesn't say anything more she looks up at Logan, totally bewildered. "Do we take your silence to mean that you don't intend divulging that name?" Logan asks stonily.

The thought has Catherine shooting out of her seat. "Well fuck that," she shouts angrily before the Inspector can reply. "We're the ones who found Harriet Leavesden, and we found the cluster of similar assaults on young males in Glywyth," she rants as she strides up and down the room, "and we also found out that Llwyd was fucking born there!" Her anger has risen to a storm of indignation and the volume of her rant has risen along with it.

Logan reaches over to close the lounge door, fearing Mrs Baines might come running in at any moment.

The Inspector clears his throat then attempts to explain. "I cannot give out the name of someone who might well be innocent." Catherine makes to protest but Logan puts up a hand and shakes his head.

"Do you really believe, Inspector, that after all the hours we have put in to finding this man, we would be so indiscreet as to risk warning him?" Even Logan's normally mild manner is being tested it seems to Catherine.

The Inspector blusters an apology. "Not at all. Not at all," he assures them, "but I can't go round accusing people before I've even investigated the matter."

"And what about Catherine?" Logan asks his tone now crisp and demanding. "While you are busy protecting a likely murderer, who is going to protect Catherine if he comes after her next?"

Catherine lets out a sharp gasp, a hand going to her throat.

"Bloody hell," Logan borrows one of Catherine's familiar oaths and crosses the room to put his arms round her. "I'm sorry, I didn't think," he tells her as she slumps against him, "I was just trying to make the point that we really need to know."

Having heard what was being said, the Inspector asks them to be patient. "I promise, I will get back to you in the next twenty-four to forty-eight hours, but there are things that I need to look into," he affirms. "Just give me that long to be sure, and if it is him I will get back to you right away."

Catherine and Logan look at each other and nod their resigned acceptance. "Alright, Inspector," Logan tells him, "we'll be waiting.

# Chapter Eleven

Logan's home office has become a hive of activity. He is working his way down a copy of Arthur's guest list finding out the whereabouts of each guest during the time of either Sara Colson's or Harriet Leavesden's murders. It means lots of phone calls to various friends and business contacts, and calling in a few favours to get things done.

Then there is Ben – Logan himself suggested calling him in. They are so close to finding this monster, that Logan will take help from the devil himself if it means keeping Catherine safe. Ben and Catherine split the guest list in half and are both using their considerable computer skills to find any and all information on each person on it. Even Logan agrees it's worth the risk if it will help find the crazy bastard.

Ever since the phone discussion with Inspector Harper, Logan has felt a nervous tension in his gut. He had only suggested that the murderer might come after Catherine to force the Inspector's hand in revealing who his suspect is, but the idea has taken hold and Logan can't shake it.

"Jesus," Ben rubs a hand over his tired eyes and rolls his head to ease out a few kinks, "I can't believe the lifestyle of some of these rich bastards – they run their lives like robots, always this place on that day and at a certain time," he moans. "I mean," he continues to no one in particular, "look at this guy; he's got over twenty million in the bank and all he does is eat work and sleep. The highlight of his year appears to be a two week holiday in France, and he's been there for the last three years, at least." *What a moron.*

Logan's head comes up. "You're looking back three years in their financials?" he asks Ben, "Why?"

"Actually, I'm going back twenty," Ben replies. "Their financials leave a trail of where they are at any one time, and that's what we're looking to prove, right? These people rarely use cash," he explains, "and their credit cards leave a data trail that's child's play to follow."

"So, have any of them been in Glywyth, Sheriton or Moorsden at the times in question?" Logan, too, is feeling tired and his tone is more belligerent than he realises.

"I'm doing my best, alright," Ben turns to Logan, his face a picture of exhaustion and anger.

"Just stop!" Catherine stands up as both the men did. "It's four in the fucking morning and none of us has had any rest, let alone sleep." Moving over to the coffee jug, Catherine grimaces when she finds it empty. "Maybe we should take a couple of hours down?" she suggests. "Or longer, if you want?"

It becomes obvious that neither man is going to be the first to admit they need a break, so Catherine decides to leave them to it. "Ok, be heroes," she glares from one to the other, "but when you get so tired you start making mistakes, missing details that could lead to the murdering bastard, just remember why we're doing this in the first place!" Crossing to the door, she holds it open, "If he gets another victim because we did something wrong...?" Not finishing the thought Catherine allows the door to close quietly behind her.

"Wow," is all Ben says, looking at Logan with raised eyebrows.

"Compelling, isn't she?" Logan gazes after Catherine then turns back to Ben. "And she's right – I apologise for being testy, we'll all work better after a couple of hours sleep."

It is still dark when Catherine wakes just an hour later. Logan is flat out on the bed beside her, his heavy arm laying across her chest. Gazing up at the ceiling Catherine thinks over the information that she found and the niggling feeling that she has missed something continues to grow. Realising that the feeling isn't going to go away, or let her sleep, Catherine carefully lifts Logan's arm and managed to get up without waking him. Pulling on a pair of her old tracky bottoms and one of Logan's shirts, Catherine makes her way back to his office and begins going through the information looking for what she believes she has missed.

It isn't long until she finds it. Having looked through all the databases that would hold photographic ID, Catherine finds the one she has been looking for.  Her hands begin to shake, her fingers barely able to hit the right key as she zooms in on a driving licence photo of her mother's murderer.

"There you are, you fucking bastard!" A couple of tears fall on to her cheeks, but Catherine scrubs them away angrily. "You think you made my mum suffer; well, let's just see how well you stand up to a little pain when I get my fucking hands on you!" Closing the lid of her laptop, she stares at it still seeing his face. "You poxy coward – now you'll face me!"

After working all day and most of the night, it is eight-thirty before either of the two men wake. Logan yawns heavily, turns over towards Catherine only to find the bed empty. Frowning, he sits up and looks around the room. She hasn't put the dress back on that she wore yesterday, he notes, and can't believe he slept through her taking a shower and dressing.

Getting up, Logan crosses to the bathroom and finds it empty – looking around he also finds it bone dry. There is no way that anyone has taken a shower that morning and that is not like Catherine.

Not at all worried, and thinking that he will find her bent over her laptop, Logan pads barefoot to his office with just a bathrobe pulled round him.

When he enters and finds Catherine not there and her laptop shut down, the worried feeling in his gut makes itself known more intensely than ever.

"Catherine!" He goes through the whole house shouting her name. Mrs Baines comes out of the lounge having begun her cleaning routine. "Have you seen Catherine," Logan asks her, then grasps both her arms when she only shakes her head. "Wasn't she down here when you arrived?" His brown eyes are now huge and dark with worry.

His fingers are biting into her arm, but Mrs Baines makes no protest. "I arrived at seven, my usual time," she tells him, "and just assumed you hadn't got up yet. The house was quiet so I got on with my work and didn't hear a thing till you, just now." Her brows crease with worry; she took to Catherine right off. "Mr Sayers, Logan...," she speaks softly but firmly so as to calm him down, "...perhaps you should tell me what's been going on? I might be able to help."

He gives her a brief outline of the situation, Catherine's past, what they have been trying to do, and what he found when he woke up.

Mrs Baines studies Logan for a moment before stating bluntly, what she thinks. "You think she found something and has gone to follow it up – do you know what it is?" she asks, then spots Ben coming down the stairs looking very interested in Logan's answer.

"No I don't," he looks up at Ben who has stopped half way down the stairs, "can you get into her laptop and find out what she was looking at last?"

Ben nods, already turning to head up to Logan's office.

Logan turns back to Mrs Baines, "I want you to call the police and ask to speak to Inspector Harper, he's in charge of the investigation. Just explain what's happened – I know we don't know for certain that Catherine has gone after this maniac, but knowing her I think it's a high probability."

Mrs Baines nods and moves back into the lounge to make the call.

Logan takes the stairs two at a time. When he enters his office, Ben looks grim. "This is the last thing she was working on," and he turns the laptop for Logan to see, "do you know him?"

Looking carefully at the photo, Logan shakes his head. "But I think I might know who would," he tells Ben. "Is there anything more you can do here?"

Ben nods, "Catherine has already gone into his financials – I should be able to see if he's staying at a hotel or renting a property nearby."

Logan tries to clear his head to think properly. "I'm going to get dressed; if you want to come with me to Robert's house you'll be more than welcome?"

"That would be great," Ben tells him. "I'll print this photo off, and any other info I can find, then I'll be ready when you are."

When the men meet up down stairs in the hallway, they are surprised to see Mrs Baines with her coat on waiting for them. "With your permission, I'm coming with you," she tells Logan. "You might find my background in psychology useful if it comes to talking to him – he's likely to be very excitable and possibly angry that Catherine would dare to confront him."

With a grateful smile, Logan agrees, "I won't allow you to put yourself in any danger, but I would be grateful for your help and advice on handling this chap."

Catherine stands outside a house, in a row of houses that has nothing about it that says 'butchering bastard inside'. But she knows better and looking at it, imagining him still asleep, her anger is growing. No doubt he is dreaming of his next victim – has he already begun the stalking process? Has he been stalking her?

That question is answered moments later when her head is pulled painfully back by her hair. "You're a clever little girl," his deep Welsh accent almost makes her lose control of her bladder. 'That voice,' the one she heard as a child, the one that has haunted even her waking hours lately, is now being breathed directly into her ear. "I wanted to take my time with you, Catherine," he tells her. "I've been following you for the last couple of years, and very entertaining it's been," he sneers, his deep voice resonating in her head.

"I don't believe you," she grinds out between clenched teeth. "I would have smelt the shit on my shoes if you'd been anywhere near me for all that time."

Her hair might still be short, but it is long enough to allow him to grasp it tightly and pull it extremely hard. But before she can cry out his other hand clamps over her mouth and her scream of pain is effectively muffled. Catherine's eyes are wide, shocked, the memories of her mum's stifled screams echoing loudly in her head. "I'm going to enjoy you so much," his lips are right next to her ear and then his teeth bite down hard on her earlobe.

Her eyes water with the pain but this time she does not allow herself to utter even a moan. Instead, she sinks her teeth into the fleshy palm that is still covering her mouth and hears, with delight, his bellowed oath. "You fucking bitch," he is dragging her towards the house and Catherine fights him every step of the way. She knows that once he gets her inside her chances of survival will not be good.

Standing on Robert Kingsley's doorstep, Logan rings the bell and when he gets no answer, pounds the door with his fist.

It is almost nine o'clock and Robert is up and dressed, just making his way down stairs when he hears the noise.

"What's going on?" he asks his housekeeper who is approaching the door with some trepidation.

"I don't know, Mr Kingsley," she replies nervously, "but it sounds urgent, and a bit frightening," she admits.

"Not to worry, Hazel," he reassures her, "I'll get the door; you go back to what you were doing."

Glad that Mr Kingsley has taken charge, Hazel hesitates not wanting to leave him completely alone with whoever is still hammering on the front door.

Robert frowns when he looks out to see Logan Sayers frantically pacing up and down between hammering on his door. "Logan, what the hell?" he asks once the door is open and he can see his friends obvious anguish.

"I need your help, Robert," Logan thrusts out the hand that is holding the printout of the man Catherine had been looking into on her laptop. "Who is he and where does he live?"

Robert frowns down at the picture then smiles, "That's Charley Edwards, he's the manager of our Sheriton warehouse," he tells Logan, then his frown returns when his friend continues to look worried. "What is it, Logan? What do you think Charley has done?" Opening the door wider he beckons Logan inside.

"I think he may have Catherine," Logan explains, "or rather, I think Catherine may have gone after him, which amounts to more or less the same thing," he states angrily. "Either way, she's in imminent danger from the man who raped and tortured her mother to death."

Taken aback, Robert Kingsley gives a mirthless laugh. "You can't be serious," he exclaims, "Charley has worked for us for the past two years and has never been the least bit of trouble. Indeed," Robert defends, "he was promoted to manager shortly after taking the warehouse job – he's always been very efficient and good at handling the workforce. I cannot believe he is the man you're looking for."

"Just give me his address, Robert, and we'll find out for sure," Logan tells him.

But Robert isn't convinced. "I can't just give out employee's personal information, Logan, you know that." It is Robert's turn to pace as he considers his friend's request. "However, I can see that you are genuinely worried; though you've given me no sound cause as to why you should be."

Logan takes in a deep breath attempting to steady himself, then drawing himself up to his full six feet four inches, reaches out and catches hold of Robert's arm just as he is pacing by him. "This," he grinds out acidly, "is Catherine we're talking about. The woman you told me you hold in very high regard. A woman, if I'm not mistaken, you yourself would have been keen to ask out had I not been in the picture." Logan watches as the younger man has the grace to blush. "I'm begging you, Robert," his voice now low and wholly sincere, "don't let Catherine suffer because of me."

A moment later, Robert smiles. "I'm not a sore loser," he tells Logan, "if you really believe Charley has anything to do with Catherine, or her mother, I'm coming with you."

Logan instinctively makes to protest, but thinks better of it. "Come on then," he claps Robert on the back then has to reach out quickly to steady him. "Sorry, I forget my own strength sometimes."

"Yes, well," Robert frowns up at the big man, "just save it all up for Charley Edwards and stop battering those who are on your side."

Together they go out to the car and the occupants waiting inside.

"For god's sake," Ben rounds on Logan as he slides into the car, "where the hell have you been, who knows what that maniac has already done to Catherine?"

Then Robert gets in the other side. "My fault," Robert turns to Ben as he gets in the front passenger seat, "I took some convincing, but I'm on board now." He gives Logan the address and they take off at breakneck speed.

Less than ten minutes later, they are outside Charley Edwards' rented house, no signs of life or evidence of Catherine having been there.

Opening her eyes to slits, Catherine tries to look around her without giving away the fact that she is no longer out cold. Edwards beat the crap out of her once he got her indoors, but he is nowhere to be seen right now.

Hearing the clink of metal on metal, her stomach clenches with the memory of another time when she heard a similar sound, but she isn't a child anymore. Gritting her teeth, she knows it is now or never; once he ties her up it will all be over.

Wiping a hand under her bloody nose, Catherine eases her way out of a small dining room and into the kitchen. She has just slid a very large carving knife out of its block when Edwards comes into the room.

Whirling round she sees his shocked face, then the anger that gives it an ugly twist of sheer madness. "You fucking bitch," he spits out, eyes bulging with rage, "why can't you ever do what you're supposed to." He lunges forward but Catherine waves the knife threateningly.

Amazingly, she isn't afraid; the spectre of him haunting her waking life and terrifying dreams has been so much worse than this reality, Catherine realises. "Come on, Edwards," she brandishes the knife with relish now, "I want the pleasure of pushing this into your cowardly gut."

He doesn't know what to do; she can see him trying to figure out his next move having never been in this situation before.

"What's the matter, Edwards, never taken a woman on who can fight back?" She is sneering at him, baiting Edwards into making a mistake. Mentally she cocks a finger at him, willing him forwards.

"You're nothing," he screams, spittle flying as he shakes his head from side to side. "You're just another cunt who doesn't deserve to live – you're weak and worthless, you little bastard!"

Catherine can hear his insanity, and thinks she detects a clue as to where his thoughts just veered off to. "Is that what she called you?" she asks more quietly. "The cunt that gave birth to you, did she think you were a weak and worthless little bastard?"

He seems to go into himself for a split second then comes back angrier than ever. "Don't you talk about my mother," he yells and takes a step forward but stops when he again sees the sharp blade Catherine is holding. "My Grandpa told me about women like you, putting yourself about like the trollop you are," his eyes never leave the blade that is standing between him and his quarry. "The Lord has forsaken you, bitch, and he won't help you when I punish you for your shameful sins."

Catherine can see that she isn't going to hold Edwards off for much longer; he is looking insane enough to walk onto the carving knife if it means getting his hands on her.

For a brief moment, she has a flash of him doing just that, the warmth of his blood spilling over her hand and down her arm – then her blue eyes turn diamond hard and bright and her soft lips curve into a snarling imitation of a smile. "Come get me, Edwards," she taunts, her right hand waving the long blade side to side, her left held out with her fingers crooked beckoning him forward. Moving her feet into a fighting stance, she readies herself to meet his charge, and then all hell breaks loose as Logan's impressive broad shoulders break in the back door of the house.

He takes the situation in quickly and decides to stand firm. "Are you alright?" he asks seeing her bloody nose and a large bruise on her cheek that is beginning to bloom painfully.

"I'm fine," she growls not taking her eyes off Edwards or lowering the knife, "now get the fuck out! We can take care of this can't we Edwards?" she challenges and sees his answering glare and nod of acceptance. Then he pulls a sharpened screwdriver out of his back pocket and mimics her combative stance.

The next voice to speak takes them all by surprise. "You're mum wouldn't want this, Catherine," Mrs Baines' soft voice rings out in the heavy silence of the kitchen. "You can't undo her pain by making him suffer." She watches as Catherine's frown deepens and her body crouches ready to pounce. "Be true to yourself, Catherine, to the woman your mum taught you to be," Mrs Baines urges quietly, "and not what this monster is trying to make you."

Too far away to take Edward's out without risking Catherine, Logan forces himself to wait for the right moment to strike; and he is with Catherine, a knife in the gut is no more that this bastard deserves. But he doesn't want it to be Catherine that drives it home, she has already suffered enough.

"He's tortured so many innocent people over so many years," Catherine reasons bitterly, "and you want me to let this cretin live – not a chance!"

Then the decision is taken out of her hands as Edwards gives a loud yell and charges forward, the deadly sharpened point of the screwdriver aimed right at Catherine's eyes.

Logan lets out an almighty, "No!" and throws himself at Edwards.

The scuffle is chaotic; Ben and Robert have joined Mrs Baines at the backdoor, having called the police for assistance first. "What the hell...," Ben gapes, then both men lurch into the fray and try to pull the two men apart, Catherine having been pushed none too gently aside.

A cacophony of sirens sound in the street, but no one in the house either hears or takes any notice. Ben and Robert manage to restrain the still struggling Edwards when an officer with handcuffs restrains him more effectively and another helps him cart Edwards away. Hands on knees and drawing in gasping breaths, Ben and Robert laugh with relief that the fight is over and everyone has come out of it alive.

Inspector Harper speaks to his men as they leave with Edwards then moves forward the better to observe the scene. "He is the illegitimate son of Charles Llwyd," he informs them all, looking particularly at Catherine, "so, in a very real way you lead us right to him," he tells her, crouching to meet her at eye level.

"We had a number of suspects, but only one who is Welsh spoken." He takes Catherine's hand, "Based on the work you did, finding all those assaults that took place in Glywyth, we did a thorough background check and found his mother, Morganna Edwards," he looks over at Logan when Catherine still doesn't respond and receives a nod of encouragement. "Catherine," he gives her hand a squeeze, "she told us that Charles Llwyd is the father of her son, Charles Edwards, that's why their voices sound so similar," again he gives her hand a gentle squeeze but still gets no response. Looking over at Logan, the Inspector shakes his head, "I'm so sorry."

Logan crawls over to where Catherine is sat on the kitchen floor, not moving or uttering a single word. Remembering what happened to her as a child, he can only hope that she won't withdraw so entirely into herself as she had then. "Catherine...?" He moves slowly forward as the Inspector moves away and speaks quietly. "It's me, Catherine...it's Logan," he tells her and takes her hand gently in his. "It's over, now, he's gone forever and they'll never let him out." *Catherine, don't leave me – not like this.*

Barely blinking, Catherine gives no sign that she has heard a single word he's spoken, and Logan turns to Mrs Baines, a hopeless plea in his dark eyes.

Moving forward, Mrs Baines sits on the floor next to Catherine. "It's alright to grieve, Catherine," she explains and puts an arm across her shoulders to draw her in to a motherly hug. "But it isn't alright to hide from all this, even within yourself," she prompts but receives no reply.

Logan closes his eyes and lets his head fall back against a kitchen unit – after everything that has happened it is all for nothing, he is going to lose Catherine anyway. A groan of agony brings everyone's eyes to look at Logan. "You're hurt," Robert observes inanely, "oh god, Logan, the bastard stabbed you."

Another groan from Logan is all it takes, "Logan...?" He could have danced a jig at the sound of Catherine's voice, if it hadn't been for the eight-inch screwdriver sticking out of his side.

## <u>Epilogue</u>

Catherine awakes in Logan's arms, her cheek soft and warm against the hard muscle of his expansive chest. "Good morning, birthday girl," he gives her a squeeze and she groans dramatically.

"I think you just broke a couple of ribs," she tells him when she manages to refill her lungs.

"Then allow me to kiss them better." Lifting the cover, he works his way down her body to her ribs and makes Catherine laugh. "Feeling better yet?" he asks, his hands reaching up to cup her full round breasts.

Despite a sharp intake of breath, Catherine says, "Not yet," then his teeth and tongue go to work and her nipples harden abruptly. "Still hurts," she tells him then gasps when his tongue moves up to find her ear and a hand moves down to cup the growing heat between her thighs. "Holy shit," she breathes then cries out when he tips her over the edge of the first wonderful peak.

Wanting to pleasure him, as he is her, Catherine moves her hand down his spine and under his gloriously firm body. But Logan just bats her hand aside; trailing kisses from her ear to her lips, he stifles any protest.

She feels her world shift and spin when he takes the kiss so deep she is dizzy from it. "Inside me," is all she can say when their lips part, but Logan just chuckles wickedly.

"Not a chance," she hears him croon before diving back under the covers to feast hungrily all the way down her body until he reaches the apex of her already spread legs. Another knowing chuckle and then he is silent but Catherine gasps and cries out in pleasure, her responses driving him wild with the love he wants to show her.

"Logan..." she yells desperately, "for pity's sake," she pleads and is relieved to feel him making his way back up her body.

"A lady shouldn't beg," he laughs as he moves over her.

"Fuck that," she declares before moving to guide him inside her.

"I'd much rather fuck you," he tells her then thrusts into Catherine holding her hips off the bed allowing her to meet him beat for fierce beat.

Their bodies climb higher than they ever have before and just when Catherine thought she might implode she hears Logan tell her that he loves her. She loves him too, and is easy with it now; even enjoying the feelings they share. Then her body tenses to erupt and Logan says, "Marry me, Catherine, be mine forever," he begs her.

And just before falling off the edge of the world, Catherine screams her reply.

Much later, over a very late breakfast that Mrs Baines has cooked them, Catherine tries to back out of her commitment. "It doesn't count," she whispers frowning down at her scrambled eggs, "I was under duress at the time." She puts a forkful of the excellent eggs in her mouth then wags the empty fork at Logan.

"You were under me," he snickers, and she blushes bright pink.

"Will you stop," and this time she uses the fork to indicate Mrs Baines in the kitchen, "she'll hear you!"

"Good," he smiles as the woman herself walks in with a fresh jug of filter coffee.

"It's so nice to see you both happy and smiling," she tells them, then hesitates when Catherine frowns.

"That's because we have some great news," Logan tells his housekeeper, and reaches over to pat Catherine on the back as she starts to choke on her eggs. "Catherine has accepted my proposal," he grins broadly, "we're getting married." *Oh, fuck it!*

"Oh, congratulations," Mrs Baines throws her now empty hands and the tea towel she's holding over her arm up in the air, causing even Catherine to laugh at her exuberance. "It couldn't happen to a nicer couple," she says catching the tea towel and dabbing her eyes with it.

When Mrs Baines goes back into the kitchen, Catherine frowns over at Logan. "If she's so damned happy for us, why is she crying for christ's sake?"

"Then you are going to marry me?" he asks her. "I won't show you your birthday present if you don't say yes," he teases

Getting up she backs away from him. "I'll decide after I've seen my present," Catherine tosses over her shoulder as she goes ahead of him out of the conservatory and heads for the lounge.

"I knew it," he shakes his head in mock dejection, "you're just after me for my money."

They both laugh, and then Catherine says, "It's your body I'm after, I can't get enough of it," then lets out a scream as Logan tickles her ribs.

"Over here," he tells her and guides Catherine towards the large bay window.

Frowning she looks down at the floor and over to the nearby armchair. "Am I going blind or is this the tiniest birthday present on the planet?"

He moves behind her, places a large gentle hand on either side of her head, and turns her to look out of the window. "Is that big enough for you...?"

A ginormous pink bow sits atop a blue sports car, the ribbon going all the way round it. "You have got to be kidding me," she breathes, shocked and stunned and..., "I can't take that!" Turning to look up at him, Catherine shakes her head, "It's too much, Logan, I can't possibly." *Bloody Nora, a fucking car!*

His huge grin has not wavered she notes nervously. "Too late," he tells her determinedly, and holds out a set of keys. "It's in your name and everything — and I've already driven it so the garage won't take it back," he lies convincingly

"But..." Catherine turns to see Mrs Baines smiling in the doorway. "I suppose you knew all about this," Catherine accuses but can't stop the smile that is tugging reluctantly at her lips. *Honestly, ganged up on! But it is gorgeous.*

Mrs Baines nods happily. "Aren't you even going to sit in it?" she enthuses encouragingly.

Turning back to Logan, Catherine takes the keys he holds out to her. Hiding her growing excitement, she manages to frown, though none too convincingly. "I suppose it wouldn't hurt to take a look," she grumbles, then marches out to the front drive with Logan and Mrs Baines on her heels.

Walking slowly around the car, she fingers the outsized bow and laughs. "I hope you had to drive home with this on," she jibes at him playfully, "I'd have paid good money to see that, wouldn't you Mrs Baines?" and both women laugh at his uncomfortable smile.

"I had it delivered," he tells her promptly, then could have bit his own tongue off.

"So, when did you get time to drive it?" Catherine asks, knowing she has found him out. Holding on to her frown for just a moment longer she cannot bare his anxious face. "Just kidding, I love it," she tells him and flings her arms round his neck. They don't notice Mrs Baines move discreetly indoors, they are too busy enjoying the moment. "So when do I get to drive it?" she asks moving to pull out of his arms.

"How about this afternoon...?" Logan replies catching her to him and planting a noisy smacker of a kiss on her still smiling lips.

"Why this afternoon? Is there something going on that I don't know about?" Catherine imagines he probably has some sort of surprise birthday party planned.

Logan doesn't hesitate, he can't or he will lose his nerve. "Yes," he replies, his smile now tentative but still in place, "we're picking your sister up from the airport."

"WHAT!"

*****

If you have enjoyed this book please take the time to write a review at the point of purchase. Thank you.

www.susan-elle.com